SWITCHING WITCHES

MAGIC AND MAYHEM, BOOK SEVEN

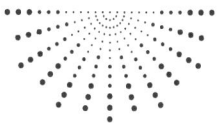

ROBYN PETERMAN

WWW.ROBYNPETERMAN.COM

Copyright © 2019 by Robyn Peterman

All rights reserved.

No part of this book may be reproduced in any form or by any electronic or mechanical means, including information storage and retrieval systems, without written permission from the author, except for the use of brief quotations in a book review.

This book is a work of fiction. Names, characters, places, and incidents either are the product of the author's imagination or are used fictitiously. Any resemblance to actual persons, living or dead, businesses, companies, events, or locales is coincidental.

This book contains content that may not be suitable for young readers 17 and under.

Cover by *Rebecca Poole of dreams2media*
Edited by *Meg Weglarz*

❦ Created with Vellum

WHAT OTHERS ARE SAYING

"If Amy Schumer and Janet Evanovitch had a baby, it would be Robyn Peterman!"
~**Dakota Cassidy**
USA Today Best Selling Author

"Funny, fast-paced, and filled with laugh-out-loud dialogue. Robyn Peterman delivers a sidesplitting, sexy tale of powerful witches and magical delights. I devoured it in one sitting!"
~**Ann Charles**
USA Today Bestselling Author
of the *Deadwood Humorous Mystery Series*

ACKNOWLEDGMENTS

While writing may be a solitary experience, I have many wonderful people who help me get my books into your hands.

My husband and kids—I love you to the moon and back. Nothing is worth it without you.

Rebecca—your covers are brilliant.
Meg—your editing has saved me from myself many times. LOL
Donna—best critique partner ever.
Wanda—I'm screwed without you.
Susan—you are a dollbaby!
Kris—you are the Blurb Guru.

DEDICATION

For Zorro.
I hope the Next Adventure will be as wonderful as this one has been.

INTRODUCTION

The Magic and Mayhem Series is an absolute delight to write. Zelda and Sassy have truly become my dysfunctional buddies. LOL Trust me… they're fun.

I hope you enjoy Switching Witches as much as I loved creating it.

BOOK DESCRIPTION

Forecast for today? Partly good witch, with a thirty-two percent chance of broom rage.

How in the Goddess's name did I get stuck at the Witchypoo Convention at Rump Arena in Hexington, Kentucky? Whoops… my bad. Rupp Arena in Lexington, Kentucky. Whatever. It's like one cavernous indoor garage sale of "magic" crap. It's nothing more than a convention of human wanna-be witches in pointy ankle boots and half-price black hats.

And where in the Goddess's gauchos did these humans get their info on witch-wear? Real witches wear Prada… and Stella McCartney.. and Alice and Olivia… and… well, you get my point.

Baba Yopaininmybutt sent me to root out the *very* evil shenanigans going down in the sea of faux witches, mummies and vamps. On the plus side, I'm looking forward to hotel sex with my hotter that heck werewolf mate. However, nookie time is nada. Believe it or not, a gay fainting goat shifter, a magical

BOOK DESCRIPTION

mystery woman and a dude who looks alarmingly like me have shown up to complicate matters.

A mystery witch is dealing in blood. I might have a twin. Where do gay fainting goat shifters come from anyway? And I will be seriously put out if I can't have hotel sex.

But I'm motivated … by multiple big O's.
Let the motherhumpin' witch-hunt begin.

CHAPTER ONE

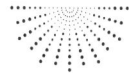

"Are you a good witch or a bad witch?" the gothic looking human disaster screeched as she body-blocked the entryway to the shitshow awaiting us. "Answer me now or prepare to be smote to the bowels of Hell where you will burn until crispy in the cauldron of eternal flame."

"Shut the front fucking door. There's a cauldron of eternal flame in Hell?" Sassy asked, baffled.

"Nope, but I'm pretty sure there's a cauldron of eternal bullshit right here," I muttered.

"Answer or be smote," the human snapped.

"Wait. Is she talking to us?" Sassy asked, trying not to laugh.

"I'd have to go with a yes on that one," I replied flatly. "The customer service here sucks."

It took everything I had not to knock the pointy black hat off of the *gatekeeper's* head. The stereotypes of witch-wear were positively cringey.

The human bared her teeth and hummed something that sounded distinctly like an out of tune version of *Ding Dong the Witch is Dead*. Her chompers looked strangely white in contrast to the jet black lipstick she sported.

What in the Goddess's name was happening? Was this seriously how humans thought witches dressed?

Glancing at the people wandering around, I sighed at the tragedy unfolding before my eyes. I'd never seen so many black robes and pointy ankle boots in my freakin' life. Mechanical flying bats zoomed overhead and sparkling black spiders hung in gauzy webs covering the windows along the long entry hallway. There were even a few live monkeys on leashes sporting spandex wings. It was like Halloween on crack.

"Good witch or bad witch?" the dummy growled. "You must declare your status to enter the sacred realm of Magical Mystery and Mayhem."

"Are those my only two options?" I inquired, clasping my hands together so I didn't zap her bald. It really wouldn't do to blow my cover in the first five minutes.

The human seemed confused. Clearly, I had strayed from the script. I was good like that.

She narrowed her bizarre blood red eyes, causing her left contact lens to pop out. It was now positioned on her cheek and looked like an inflamed boil. I considered snapping a picture with my phone but thought better of it. She was blocking the entrance and pissing her off more probably wasn't in my best interest. Normally I would wave my hand and zap her out of the building, but I wasn't allowed to reveal my magic to humans. This was sucking some serious ass so far.

Totally unaware of her newly acquired plastic facial wound, the wannabe witch rudely cleared her throat and pointed her wand at me. "Don't make me put a curse on you," she hissed, waving the useless glittery stick in a figure eight motion. "Are you a good witch or a bad witch?"

Glancing over at Sassy—my BBF by default—I shrugged and rolled my eyes.

"What did you expect?" Sassy asked, trying to peek past the weird human guard dog. "The place is called Rump Arena."

"Dude, it's Rupp Arena—not Rump Arena." My second eye roll encompassed both Sassy and the idiot at the door. I didn't have time for this crap. It was ludicrous enough that we were even here.

"Rupp, Rump, whatever," Sassy replied, turning her attention to the faux witch standing in our way. "My BFF is an *in-between* witch. I'm working on myself so I'd have to say I'm a good witch eighty-two percent of the time. A bad witch forty-seven percent of the time and a cranky witch sixty-one percent of the time. However, standing here and staring at your skanky-ass witch costume will increase the odds on my cranky witch status, which in turn will make my bad witch probability escalate. This is not ideal if you want to keep your hair. You feel me?"

"Duuuuude," I said with a laugh as I slapped Sassy a high five. "That was impressive."

"Right?" Sassy shot back with a shrill giggle. "I was speaking German with a little Chinese thrown in."

"I'm so confused," our witchy human buddy replied, staring at us like we might be contagious.

"I get that all the time," Sassy told her in all seriousness. "I speak in tongues. Most of the time I don't even realize I'm speaking another language. It's completely unbelievable!"

The human quickly grabbed her clipboard and moved behind the table loaded down with badges shaped like little black cats. "Okaaay… right. Names?"

"Sassy Louise Bermangoggleshitz Pants."

"Zelda."

"Last name?" the flustered meanie asked me, probably wishing she'd volunteered for a different job.

"Zelda's last name is Houston or Dallas," Sassy told the woman and then winked and grinned at me. "Do you have a name?"

The human nodded and kept shuffling through her papers. I

assumed she was looking for our names which I was positive were nowhere on her list. Our fearless and clearly unorganized leader, Baba Yaga, hadn't mentioned we needed to register for the *Witchypoo Convention*. When we got back home to Assjacket, West Virginia, I was going to kick our idiotic boss's ass for sending us to this debacle.

"I'm Verruca Trotcackler," she replied, still pouring over her list.

"Are you shitting me?" I choked out. "For real?"

Verruca's eyes narrowed and she yanked a small glass vial from the pocket of her shapeless black robe. "Yessssss," she snapped, wielding her bottle and grabbing her wand. "I have eye of newt in this bottle and I'm not afraid to use it. If you value your life, you will not tangle with Verruca Trotcackler. I am the most powerful spellcaster in Kentucky—or at least in Lexington—or *Hex*ington, as I like to call it. And by the way, *Zelda Houstonordallas* is a stupid witch name."

"Take. That. Back," I said so calmly that Sassy dove underneath the badge table in terror. Of course, my last name was not Houstonordallas, but that was irrelevant. No one was going to smack talk me like that—especially not a human dressed in a shitty witch costume.

Verruca's one red eye and one brown eye grew wide with fear. I was ninety-nine point nine percent sure that my hair had begun to blow around my head and that a few enchanted sparkles might have leaked from my fingertips.

Thankfully, everyone here was so nutty that *my* normal didn't stand out.

For the love of the Goddess, there was a practically naked human man painted silver posed in a frozen position not even ten feet away. Not to mention, there was a magician sawing a gal in half down the hallway.

Sassy and I fit in perfectly. We just needed to keep a lid on the big stuff. Zapping a wart or two onto Verruca's nose should be fine.

"Sorry," Verruca mumbled. "I can't seem to find your names on the list."

"They're right there," I said pointing to the list and wiggling my finger.

Sure enough *Sassy Louise Bermangoggleshitz Pants* and *Zelda Houstonordallas* appeared at the top. Verruca gasped and stared at me like I had three heads. I didn't. I had one head of fabulous wild red hair.

And… I was a *real* freakin' witch.

"Strange," Verruca said, gaping at our names. "I could have sworn… I mean… umm…"

"Your contacts must have blurred your vision," I told her politely. I could be nice—kind of. There was no reason to send Verruca to therapy… yet. "Oh look! There are our badges."

I snapped my fingers and conjured up kitty badges for Sassy and me. And while I was at it, I conjured up one for my mate Mac and one for Sassy's mate Jeeves.

"Weird," Verruca said, as she warily handed them over to me. "Did you bring your familiars?"

Yanking Sassy out from under the table, I slapped her badge on her chest. "You mean my Crotch Goblins?"

"Your *what*?"

"My Crotch Goblins. And yes, I brought them. There are three—Fat Bastard, Jango Fett and Boba Fett. They're cats with ball cleaning issues. I'm quite sure they're down the hall taking bets on if the woman getting sawed in half will live. Oh, and don't be alarmed if they talk. They've had electronic voice boxes inserted. The program has been set to profane. Just ignore them."

"Is that humane?" Verruca asked, paling at the new information.

"No, but it's funny," I told her as I moved to go past her. I had to congratulate myself on that one. There was no way in the Goddess's green earth that my cats could pretend to be real cats. Talking cats would be a dead giveaway. "And don't threaten them with eye of newt. They'll eat it."

"Okay," Verruca said, shoving the bottle back into her pocket. "The vendors are all open and take credit cards, but most prefer cash. Your badge will get you into all the parties and lectures. However, if you want your palm read by Marie Laveau, you have to pay… in blood."

"You're joking." I halted my forward motion and glared at Verruca.

If true, this was a disturbing wrinkle and possibly the reason we were here. Baba Yocrypticpaininmyass wasn't too forthcoming about this mysterious mission. But blood? Bartering for blood was forbidden, as was stealing hair. For a witch—a *real* witch—taking human or magical blood was a big fat no-no. Even just a drop was illegal. Interesting.

However, someone sporting the name Marie Laveau was definitely *not* a real witch. The *real* Voodoo Queen by that name was as dead as a doornail.

"Not joking," Verruca said, holding up her Band-Aided middle finger. "She doesn't take much."

Sassy gasped and began to sparkle. Not good. I wasn't sure if it was because Verruca had flipped us off or it was the blood thing. It didn't matter. Sassy was capable of blowing up Rump Arena… shit, Rupp Arena. That certainly wouldn't go over too well.

Clapping my hands and stunting Sassy's magic, I smiled at Verruca. "Does the health department know about this *bloodletting*?"

Verruca did not smile back. "It's all in fun," she protested, growing uncomfortable under my gaze.

"Real witches don't deal in blood, Verruca," I snapped. "Ever."

Her eyes narrowed and she pursed her black lips unattractively. "How would *you* know? Someone dressed in Prada is not a *real* witch. I know a real witch when I see one."

Sassy grunted and raised her hands high in the air. Verruca was about to lose a body part—or gain one. I could never tell with Sassy. Shooting Sassy a look that made her reconsider barricading herself back under the table, she reluctantly let her hands fall to her sides.

Breathing in through my nose and slowly out through my mouth, I got up in Verruca's face. She was treading on some very thin ice. I took my fashion *very* seriously. "It's Stella McCartney. Not Prada. I only wear Prada on Tuesdays, Valencia Snotcracker."

"Ohhhh, good one," Sassy congratulated me.

"Thank you," I replied. "And Veronica, you should seriously get your eyes checked."

"Why?" she snapped.

"Because you clearly can't tell the difference between a real witch and a fake one."

On that note, we entered the sacred realm of Magical Mystery and Mayhem. It was a shit show of epic proportions. There were enough counterfeit witches, vampires and mummies walking around to give me nightmares for the next century or two—but there was also real magic somewhere in the mass of ridiculousness.

Maybe there was a reason to check this out. Or maybe Baba Yaga was right out of her debatably sane mind.

But then again, what the Hell did I expect? She did send us to the *Witchypoo Convention* at *Rump* Arena in *Hexington*, Kentucky…

Let the witch-hunt shenanigans begin.

CHAPTER TWO

Two days earlier...

"Houston, we have a problem," Baba Yaga grumbled as she paced erratically across the hardwood floor in the great room of the home Mac and I shared.

I loved my house. It was my safe haven—full of love, light and magic. Baba Yaga was screwing with my chi by simply breathing in it at the moment. Even the fact that she'd quoted the fantabulous movie, *Apollo 13*, wasn't going to make me cut her a break. Of course, the leader of all Witches now lived in *my* territory of Assjacket, West Virginia—*with my dad, no less*—and liked to drop by unannounced with annoying regularly. That alone was enough to make me consider moving.

However, miracle of miracles, here I was in Assjacket, West Virginia, happier than I'd ever been in my thirty-one years—a fact that gave me nightmares occasionally. I had Mac, my mate and the most gorgeous werewolf on the planet.

We had two perfectly beautiful twin babies, Audrey and Henry. I'd been terrified my babies would come out as puppies due to the fact that I was in a cross-species relationship, but thank the Goddess, they hadn't. All of the violent threats I'd made to Mac's joystick during labor were for naught—which was a good thing. I loved his joystick.

"Goddess in mom jeans," I muttered to myself, wincing at Baba Yaga's appalling choice of outfit. "I don't have time for this today."

Not only did I have plans to get laid, I had to go into the office and make sure none of my idiot townsfolk were bleeding or broken.

My job as the Shifter Whisperer, or *Shifter Wanker* as I preferred to be called, kept me busy because Shifters were extremely accident-prone. I complained constantly so my reputation as an uncaring, materialistic witch stayed secure, but sadly it was being shredded systematically. Everyone thought I was nice, good and kind. It was freakin' horrible.

Dealing with a certifiable Baba Yaga on a daily basis made me want to blow something up, but luckily, most of Assjacket was still standing—so far.

"I repeat," Baba Yaga hissed as she began to march in tight little circles, making me slightly dizzy. "Houston, we have a problem."

Baba Yaga's turbulent movement didn't faze me a bit, but the way she was dressed alarmed me greatly and made my stomach clench in terror. Something was wrong. The Almighty Leader of the Witches was usually clad in horrifying 80's attire like a perfectly awful Madonna wannabe.

Not today. Today Baba Yaga—aka Carol aka the woman shacking up with my father, much to my chagrin—was wearing what I could only describe as a *housecoat*. The housecoat had no sequins, no feathers, it wasn't even remotely sheer and it wasn't low cut. Baba Yaga's famous cleavage was nowhere in sight. And her blonde hair? It was *flat*. Actually, it looked nice, but it was all kinds of wrong. It was normally teased a mile high and sprayed within an inch of its life.

Shit.

"For the love of everything that rides a broom," Sassy groused with an enormous eye roll, clearly untroubled by our leader's unusual outfit. "We've already established that Zelda's name is *not* Houston. Wait... unless it *is* Houston. Did you change it and not tell me?"

My eye roll beat hers. "No. No, I did not."

"Okay, good," Sassy said with a nod that made her mass of blonde curls bounce. "However, if you do decide to change it, I say go with Dallas instead of Houston."

"Because?" I inquired, automatically asking a question that I actually didn't want the answer to. Sassy had the ability to render me speechless... and mindless. Often. She was my BFF —by default—although I did love her. Caring about people was still somewhat new to me, but Sassy had grown on me like a fungus that didn't require medication.

Spending nine months in the magical pokey together for misuse of magic, among other things, had been eye opening. I'd wanted to zap her bald regularly. Well, I did zap her bald a few times, but I was working on my control now. My success rate was hovering at around twenty percent.

"Better shopping in Dallas," Sassy replied.

Since she was correct, I decided she could keep her hair.

"Are you done?" Baba Yaga demanded of Sassy just as Baba's sister Marge poofed into the room in a blast of cookie-scented wind and glitter.

The day had gone from weird to weirder—par for the course in my life.

Marge's outfit gave Baba Yaga's a run for the money. My stomach took another dive as I checked her out. Something terrible was afoot.

Normally, Cookie Witch, better known as Marge, was

impeccably dressed in the latest fashion. Today it was sweatpants, flip-flops and a starched t-shirt. Very unsettling.

Right now the two most powerful witches in existence were freaking out in my living room. This did not bode well for me getting to play out a pornographic fairy tale with Mac this afternoon while the twins took their nap.

"Have you told them?" Marge demanded as she began to pace the room with her deranged sister.

The direction of the conversation was making me itchy. Baba Yaga and Cookie Witch were only semi-sane on a good day. Today wasn't turning out to be good.

"Told us what?" I asked.

"Well," Baba Yaga said, wringing her hands as plain, ugly brown house slippers appeared on her feet. "It seems that there are some issues at the Witchypoo Convention."

"Repeat," I said, trying not to laugh. Baba Yaga had a rep a bit like Mother Nature from the TV commercial... she didn't like to be laughed at. Her heinous slippers were worrisome, but I was having a difficult time getting past *Witchypoo*.

"Issues," she snapped, narrowing her eyes at me.

"Nope, got that part," I said, staring at my fingernails. Damn, I needed a manicure. "The other part."

"There are issues at the Witchypoo Convention," she repeated.

I now was tying my shoelaces on shoes that had no laces and biting down on my lip. Hard. She had to be joking— although she rarely joked. The *Witchypoo Convention*?

"Goddess in a tube top," Sassy yelled and threw her hands in the air accidentally blowing up the lamp she was standing next to. "That's disgusting. Why in the world is there a witch poop convention? That is *private business*. I would never poop with a bunch of witches watching. I can't even poop if I'm not at home. Makes long shopping trips a little difficult. However, I can poop at my friends' houses and at the Assjacket Diner if no one else is in the bathroom."

And silence ensued. Sassy was a lethal weapon of mass confusion.

Baba Yaga was the first to regain the power of speech after Sassy's unappetizing diatribe. "You really think Sassy taking over for you is a good plan?" she asked Marge.

"I never said it was a *good* plan. I just said it was a plan," Marge replied, shaking her head. "And you think Zelda will do your job justice?"

"I can answer that," I chimed in, glaring at both of the witches-in-charge who were now magically sporting pink sponge rollers in their hair. That almost made me run for cover. It was so incredibly out of the realm of normal, but I had to deal with the matter at hand first. "No. The answer is no. I will not do justice to being the next Baba Yaga because I have no intention of taking the job. I'm the Shifter Wanker. I heal dumbass Shifters. They're as clumsy as the Goddess on fucking roller skates. I'm good at it and I like it. However, that is top-secret information. My rep as an uncaring materialistic witch has taken so many freakin' hits in Assjacket that it gives me gas."

"I bet they fart at the poop convention too," Sassy added with a gag.

Waving my hand, I clamped Sassy's lips together. We needed to figure out why Carol and Marge looked like Hell on a stick. Did their offensive outfits mean the world was coming to an end? Goddess, that would suck. I was sure I wasn't going to like the real answer, but since I was now a mother to two beautiful witch slash werewolf babies, I was trying to be mature. Mature witches got to the bottom of problems—even ones that had to do with absurd things like *Witchypoo* conventions and petrifying ensembles.

"First off, I'd like to go on record saying that I was clueless witches even have conventions. And whoever named the convention *Witchypoo* should be zapped on the ass until they can't sit for a month," I announced.

"It's not a *real* witch convention," Marge informed me. "It's a fake witch convention—filled with humans who like to dance naked around campfires and pretend that wands and brooms actually work."

Sassy snapped her fingers and stretched her mouth back out. "So no public pooping?"

"Goddess, no," Baba Yaga said, scrunching her nose. "While it *is* a fake witch convention, it's come to our attention that some real witches might be in attendance."

"And that's a problem?" I asked, not following.

So what if witches were mixing with humans? As long as they didn't reveal themselves, it wasn't a big deal.

Baba and Marge exchanged loaded glances.

"*Shenanigans*," Marge said, sounding very grave.

Again, I wanted to laugh. Again, I didn't. I wasn't in the mood to have my ass zapped.

"And the real witches are causing *shenanigans*?" I asked, barely keeping a straight face.

We lived a secret life in public. No human knew about the incredible magical realm living among them in their own world. Witches, Shifters, Vampyres and unfortunately, the occasional Demon walked around undetected everywhere on the Goddess's green earth.

"We think so," Baba Yaga confirmed.

"So do something about it," I said with an eye roll. Why in the Goddess's gauchos were they dressed like bag ladies and stomping around my house in a tizzy? Carol and Marge were not ones to suffer idiots lightly. The scar on my butt could attest to that.

"Excellent idea!" Marge said with far too much enthusiasm for my liking.

"Okay, great," I said, pushing both of them towards the front door. "I have an appointment with a few orgasms in an hour or so... so you guys have fun."

"Not so fast," Baba Yaga said in a voice that made me narrow my eyes. "We are already doing something about it... even as we speak."

"To be more accurate," Marge chimed in with a smile that made me slightly ill, "*you two* will be doing something about it."

"Count me out. I *will not* poop in public," Sassy announced, crossing her arms over her chest and stomping her foot. "Focal matters are not my thing."

"Fecal," I corrected her and then winced.

"Is that Swedish?" Sassy asked, looking confused.

"Umm... yes," I replied. It was better to just go with the flow with Sassy. If she got too confused things started to explode. I'd already lost a lamp.

"That's what I thought," she said with a curt nod as she produced a notebook from thin air and wrote the word down. "I'm not fluent in Swedish yet. But back to my point... I have a very active gag reflex—but not with blowjobs. I'm excellent with blowjobs. My husband slash mate slash sex god, Jeeves, can confirm this. However, my adopted chipmunk Shifter sons are not very good at flushing so I've hurled several times in just the last week alone. You have no idea how horrifying it is to find out one of your chipmunks busted a grumpie without the common courtesy to flush the steamer. I considered waxing the fur off of all four of them, but figured that would send them to therapy more than the three times a week that they're already going at the moment. I've solved the issue by requiring them release their chocolate hostages in the woods from now on. If they can't flush their dookies, they can lay cable in the forest."

"Sassy," I snapped, holding on to my sanity and the need to zap her into next year by a thread.

"Yes, Zelda?"

"No one poops at this convention."

"So they all just hold it?" she asked, perplexed. "That can't be healthy."

"And I repeat," Baba Yaga said dryly to Marge. "Sassy is a good choice of replacement for you?"

"I didn't choose. The Goddess did and you well know it," Marge huffed. "At least I don't have a replacement who refuses to take the job."

"Whoa," Sassy said, eyeing Marge. "I can refuse?"

"No," Marge shouted, making everyone in the room jump.

Sassy shrugged and sighed. "Okay. I was just checking."

I closed my eyes and said a quick prayer to the Goddess. If the Goddess really had chosen Sassy and me, she was losing her marbles. The title of Baba Yaga was bestowed upon a witch who was strong enough and wise enough to lead our kind. I was definitely strong enough as I had both light and dark magic within me. Light because all witches were born that way. And the dark? Well, that was compliments of my mother; who, thanks to me, had no power at all now. My wicked mother was living out what was left of her very evil life as a human.

But wise? No one would call me wise.

I was constantly working on my own mothering skills since I'd had the world's suckiest maternal parental unit. At least I'd found my dad, even though I did *accidentally* run him over with my car when we first met... which was part of the reason for my stay in the pokey with Sassy.

Fabio aka Fabdudio aka my dad had no clue about me until I was grown. When he found out and tried to find me, he'd let my mother put a curse on him to protect my life. He'd ended up as my mangy cat until I told him I loved him and broke the curse. Kind of weird but somehow appropriate. He was turning into the best dad in the Universe and I adored him.

The fact that my mother wanted to kill me kept our town therapist, Roger the rabbit Shifter's bank account very healthy. However, since coming to Assjacket, I'd learned that I was lovable and I could love other people. I suppose if I hadn't gone through what I'd gone through I wouldn't be where I was right now. And I loved where I was right now. I didn't want to add anything to it—especially not the title Baba Yaga.

"Zelda, it's about time you accepted your fate," Baba Yaga said with a raised brow and a hint of a smile. "You have minions."

"I'd hardly call Sleepy, Doc, Sneezy, Grumpy and Sponge Bob *minions*. They're massive fucking trees," I snapped.

Of course, they did come when I bid them, but they made one Hell of a mess. Moving trees resulted in torn up yards. They were sneaky enormous freaks of nature. It was some kind of poetic fucked up justice that I would end up with destructive trees as minions considering I had enough power in my pinky finger to blow up the entire United States. Every night the leafy bastards would replant themselves in a different order and then laugh hysterically when I called them by the wrong names. The only thing that kept me from chopping them into firewood was that they adored Henry and Audrey. Sponge Bob had even cut some of his own branches to make two baby swings.

"It's not like you have to take over *yet*," Marge pointed out. "Sassy is still learning how to use the potion to keep the magical balance in the world even."

"And I still need to learn to speak Canadian," Sassy added very seriously. "I can't understand a dang thing they say. It would be very irresponsible of me to hold a job where I couldn't communicate with my employees."

Again, Sassy rendered us mute. I considered explaining to her the Canadians spoke the same language we did but decided against it. That could take days and I still had hopes of getting laid in an hour.

"Color me confused," I said, shaking my head. "If you two horribly dressed witches are still in charge, then why do we have to go check on the shenanigans?"

Baba Yaga shrugged and laughed. "Because Marge and I are too recognizable. If there *are* shenanigans, the witches responsible will run if they catch wind that we're there. Sooooo... since the Goddess clearly went on a bender or four when she chose you girls, we've decided that you shall represent us."

As she finished her explanation both she and Marge were suddenly wearing shower caps and had bright green facial masks on. It was simply too fucking much.

"Sweet Goddess in a thong," I shouted, covering my eyes. "If you'll stop with the appalling transformation we'll do it. I'm gonna need eye bleach soon."

"Wonderful," Baba Yaga purred victoriously.

I didn't like her tone at all.

"So we're like undercover Baba Yaga and undercover Cookie Witch? We're switching witches?" Sassy asked, warming to the idea.

"Yes," Marge said, clapping her hands together with delight.

In the flash of an eye, Marge's horrible outfit was gone and she was back to her normal self in a killer Chanel sheath.

"Do I get to wear your clothes?" Sassy asked, getting more excited by the second.

"Absolutely!" Marge said. "I have a brand new hot pink Prada sundress that I haven't even worn yet."

Sassy's scream of delight made me slap my hands over my ears. What came next was so terrifying it was hard to explain.

"And you can peruse my closet, Zelda," Baba Yaga told me as she wiggled her nose and went from the housecoat look to utterly horrifying—but at least it was the kind of horrifying outfit I was used to and comfortable with.

Our stuck-in-the-eighties leader was now back to her gag-inducing self. She wore a lime green spandex bodysuit coupled with a silver sequined cone bra and topped off with hair teased so high a bird could make six nests in it. At least a hundred black rubber bracelets adorned each wrist and a feathered stretchy headband was plastered around her head. Her ruffled skirt was a sheer gauzy orange and she had on Converse high-tops. I almost puked in my mouth. But the most shocking part was even though the attire was stupefying, the woman was still otherworldly gorgeous.

"No," I choked out. "I'm good. Besides, I'm rough on clothes. Spandex makes me hurl and I'd hate to return your wardrobe all smelly."

"Fine point," Baba Yaga said with a nod as she took Marge's hand in hers and turned to leave. "You'll be leaving the day after tomorrow. We'll have a few lessons tomorrow morning."

On that cryptic note, Baba Yaga—aka Carol—snapped her fingers and poofed away with a grinning Marge.

"I think we just got played," I said, waving my hand to dissipate the glitter they'd left behind.

"Pretty sure you're right," Sassy agreed. "But I'm gonna look killer in pink Prada."

"At least I don't have to wear a cut up sweatshirt with leggings and a headband," I muttered.

"And thank the Goddess, we don't have to poop in public."

Well, there was that.

CHAPTER THREE

"The Witchypoo Convention? Seriously?" Mac asked with a grin as he gently wiped the applesauce out of Henry's hair.

"Yep," I replied, lifting Audrey out of her highchair and planting a big wet smooch on her chubby cheek. "Sassy and I got sucker-punched by Baba Yodorko and have to go figure out the witchy shenanigans."

Mac paused in thought for a moment as Henry joyously applied more applesauce to his red curls. "Jeeves and I will accompany you. We can check in with the local Shifter pack and see if they've noticed anything unusual."

"You know what *that* means?" I asked as a wide grin pulled at my lips.

Mac squinted at me and smiled even though my beautiful man had no clue where my mind was headed. "Umm…. Nope."

"Hotel sex," I squealed, doing a mostly uncoordinated dance around the room much to Audrey and Henry's delight.

"Smeeeeeeex!" Henry squealed, blowing an applesauce raspberry and pumping his little arms over his head. "Yayayayayayayayay!"

I froze in mortification and closed my eyes. I loved my children more than I ever knew I could love anyone or anything. I would happily and willingly die for them. I was also clearly giving them daily reasons to need therapy—decades of therapy.

Shitshitshit.

"Noooo," I choked out, desperately trying to save the day… or at least the moment. "Mommy said *hex*. Like a magic trick."

"Like dis?" Audrey asked as she wiggled her little fingers and doused Henry in so much applesauce that it was difficult to tell he was a toddler.

"Yummy," Henry grunted as he ate his way out of the spell his twin sister had performed.

And not to be outdone by his sibling, he sliced his small arm through the air and made chocolate chips rain down from the ceiling—thousands of chocolate chips.

"Smexy hexy," Henry bellowed with pride.

Our babies were two of a kind—literally. Never in our history had there been twin witch-werewolves. They were both redheaded healer witches like me and could shift into werewolves with a magical affinity for the earth like Mac. The Goddess had blessed Henry and Audrey with unimaginable gifts, which scared the crap out of me. Time would only tell how powerful our little goofballs would turn out to be.

"No more," Mac said sternly, trying not to laugh. "Clean this up, you two."

With sad little sighs, Henry and Audrey clapped their hands and the food fight was over, except for a few chocolate chips that I'd swiped for later.

"Okay, loves of my life," I said as I put Audrey on the floor. "It's naptime. Do you wanna fly to your room or ride daddy?"

"Ride Daaaaddy!" Henry shouted with glee as he toddled across the room towards Mac like a tiny drunken sailor.

Mac grinned and shifted effortlessly to his wolf. The beauty and simplicity of his transition still took my breath away. He was huge and a shiny chocolate brown. His sapphire eyes were exactly the same color in his human form as in his wolf form. Mac nudged our giggling children with his wet nose and they immediately climbed on board.

"Run, daddy!" Audrey squealed as she grabbed his fur and bounced on his back.

"Fast, daddy," Henry added.

Mac was not one to deny his babies anything, so fast it was. I grinned as they zipped out of the kitchen screaming with laughter. My life had turned out so fantastic it unnerved me. However, Roger, my porno loving rabbit therapist, told me that I deserved it and to enjoy every moment.

I was working on that.

Although, Henry, Audrey and Mac made it pretty dang easy to enjoy the moments.

"They're asleep," Mac announced in a whisper.

"How much time does that give us?" I asked as I whipped my dress over my head and went for my platform wedges.

"Leave the shoes on. They make my dick hard," Mac said, tearing his t-shirt apart in his haste to remove it. "They conked out fast, so I'd say we have forty-five minutes to an hour and a half."

"Should I elongate my hair so we can play Rapunzel?" I questioned as I raced around the great room and closed all the shutters.

"No time," Mac grunted as he pulled off his jeans and boxer briefs in one move. "Maybe we could act out Goldilocks and the Wolf."

"That's Red Riding Hood and the Wolf," I corrected him with a giggle.

"Right," he replied with a sexy lopsided grin that made me tingle all over. "All of my blood is residing in my Bon Jovi at the moment—not thinking real clearly."

"I could whip up the granny cap and glasses."

He paused and considered. "We played that last night. I say we switch it up."

"The Little Mermaid?" I suggested.

"We flooded the house the last time we tried that one," Mac pointed out as he began to stalk me like prey.

It was all kinds of hot. I kept darting around the room so he would have to chase me.

"The Lion King?" I proposed as I wiggled my nose and flew to the other side of the room just as he was about to pounce on me.

"That's kind of weird," he said, grinning like a fool as he moved across the room faster than could be tracked with a human eye and pinned me happily against the wall.

"What would you suggest we play?" I purred as I rubbed my naked body against his.

The sound he made deep in his throat was so sexy my knees almost buckled.

"How about the Witch and the Werewolf?" he inquired as his fangs dropped and his eyes glowed with desire.

"I don't think I know that one," I whispered and then moaned as his hands began to expertly explore my overheated body. "How do we play it?"

"It's very hard," Mac said with a chuckle, jutting his hips forward so I could feel just how *hard* it was. "Would you like to hear the story, little witch?"

"Do you think you'll still be able to speak in two minutes?" I shot back, taking his enormous and gorgeous length in my hands and stroking it.

"Possibly," he hissed out as pleasure made him drop his head back to his shoulders.

"Should I stop so you can tell me the story?" I teased with a naughty grin.

"Umm… no," he said gruffly, grabbing my hand and holding it in place. "I think it will enhance the length and size of the story."

The giggle that erupted from my throat was quickly silenced with a kiss that left me dizzy. It was all kinds of insane that sex with Mac kept getting better and better. Sex was great. Love plus sex made it freakin' fabulous.

"Goddess, I love you," he said as his eyes searched my face like he was memorizing it.

I shivered and it wasn't because I was naked except for my fabulous Jimmy Choo wedges. Mac's expression caused my shudder. His lids were hooded and his lust unmistakable. His breathing was heavy and his body tense with desire.

"You are gorgeous," I whispered, running my fingertips through the light sprinkling of dark hair on his chest.

"Not nearly as gorgeous as you are," he replied as his lips found my collarbone and began to slide lower.

I arched back wantonly as he latched onto my nipple. The firm pulls from his lips went straight to my toes and the moan that left my mouth begged for more.

He smelled like heaven—all soapy and sexy. He pulled back and stared at me with so much love and adoration in his eyes that I wanted to cry. My heart was heavy in my throat as he traced my bottom lip with his finger and watched his motion with intensity.

"I don't think we should fuck," he said.

"Wait." I squinted at Mac and pursed my lips. "I'm not sure I like this story anymore. And I'd like to point out with all the blood hanging out in your Bon Jovi instead of your brain, you should not be thinking at all. You feel me?"

"Let me explain," he said as scooped me up and tossed me

onto the couch. "We are definitely going to fuck, but not until I've made love to every inch of your sexy body."

"Oh my Goddess, that's so freakin' hot," I gasped out, beginning to like the story—a lot.

"I am pretty hot," he agreed with a sexy smirk.

"Well, you're certainly obnoxious and confident," I shot back with a delighted laugh.

Mac flexed his ridiculously and perfectly muscled arms like an idiot and grinned. "I'm confident that you're gonna come so hard you'll pass out."

"You sure about that, werewolf?" I challenged, loving how goofy my sexy man was.

"I don't make promises I can't keep, little witch. Never have, never will."

My heart beat with excitement so loudly in my chest I was sure he would hear it. "I dare you."

"My pleasure," he replied with a raised brow and a chuckle.

He lowered his head between my legs and held me motionless as I gasped and tried to move. My hips wanted to thrust, but his hands held me still. The sensation was so intense I wanted to scream.

"Goddess, Mac," I hissed as my body verged on orgasm.

"I prefer God, but Goddess will work in a pinch."

He had no intention of stopping and used his fingers and tongue in ways I didn't know were legal. Grabbing a pillow from the couch, I slammed it over my face to muffle my screams. My screams made Mac intensify his efforts. Glittering golden sparkles rained down gently around us as I was unable to hold back my magic. I trembled and cried out under his expertise.

"Is this the part of the story where we do the deed?" I gasped out as a heat coiled between my legs and the pressure threatened to undo me.

"Gettin' there, baby," he said gruffly as he continued

making magic with his fingers, causing stars to burst across my vision. "It would be a real shame to rush to the end of the story."

Goddess, he was a dick—a sexy, well-hung wanker.

"I'm pretty sure we're close to the end of the story," I insisted as I pressed my legs together to trap his hand and keep it where I wanted it.

"Beg," he demanded as he lowered his head to my breast and nipped.

"Witches don't beg, werewolf," I shot back as my hips undulated and belied my words.

"Today they do. That's in the story, witch."

"Who made this story up?" I demanded as my body danced to a carnal rhythm, begging for more.

"I did," he replied with a laugh.

His mouth replaced his fingers and he bit down and then sucked. The orgasm ripped through me like a tornado. My body thrashed and twisted with absolute joy. Mac never stopped and ramped me right back to the place where I was out of control.

"Beg," he hissed as he ran his tongue from my belly to my aching breasts.

"Fuck me, wolf," I whispered.

"Can't hear you, witch," he ground out and positioned his cock against my wet and needy opening.

"Do me now or I'll turn you into a toad," I hissed as he pushed the head of his cock into me.

"Not sure that's part of the story," he said with a grin.

"Sorry. My bad. I was improvising. Just do me. If the twins wake up your balls will be so blue, they'll fall off your body."

"Good point," he said, pushing a little farther into my body. "So fucking perfect," he ground out and then stilled.

The feeling of fullness was like a drug I couldn't live

without. I dug my nails into his broad shoulders and tried to push my body onto his, but he held me fast.

He continued to rotate his hips and nipped at my neck. Mac's fangs initially scared me silly but were now a *serious* turn on. I wanted him to slam his body into mine and bite me. He needed to get to the good part of the story and just fuck me.

"Pretty sure we're at the end of the story," I told him as I arched and rubbed my breasts against his chest.

His quick harsh intake of breath was way hotter than August in Assjacket, West Virginia. I grinned and tightened my body around the part of him that was inside me and squeezed hard. His sexy muttered curse was exactly what I wanted to hear and I contracted around him again.

"Son of a bitch," he growled and buried himself to the hilt with a swift thrust.

He was almost too big to handle, but my body softened immediately. I closed my eyes and vivid colors danced across my vision as he began to move. My hips joyously met each deep thrust as he powered his way into my body, heart and soul.

"Slow or fast?" he ground out as the muscle in his jaw worked overtime.

"Fast. We're parents, for the love of the Goddess. Slow is for childless couples."

"I'm on it."

The speed of his thrusts increased and he began to fuck me like the animal he was. It was so incredible, I felt like I was floating. My magic continued to dance around us and the great room looked like a pornographic fairy tale come to life. I gasped in astonishment as he withdrew from my body, but before I could say a word in protest he flipped me over to my hands and knees and slammed back into me.

"Need to be closer," he growled as he tangled his fingers in my wild hair and held me where he wanted me. "You're perfection."

"Not even close," I said as I fell forward onto my outstretched arms, giving him even better access to my body.

"Perfect for me," he hissed as his speed ramped up to something that should have sent us to the Next Adventure.

I loved his possession of my body and pumped back against his thrusts sending us both into a wild frenzy. The power of rational thought deserted me as an explosive orgasm tore through my body. Mac howled as he joined me.

I felt like I was falling down the rabbit hole as waves of tingling pleasure consumed me. For a second everything turned black.

"I think I passed out," I said with surprise.

"Told ya," Mac replied with total male satisfaction. "Pretty damned good story."

I rolled my eyes and giggled. He certainly didn't break his promises. The story was damned good. Mac rolled us to our sides. Still buried deep inside me, he spooned me and kissed my hair and neck.

"You are my everything, Zelda," he whispered.

"And you're mine, Mac," I said, snuggling close. "Do you think we have time for another story before Henry and Audrey wake up?"

"I certainly think we could try," he said as I felt him harden again inside my body.

We had time for two more stories. The kids took a very long nap.

The day had started horribly and ended perfectly.

As of now, Mac was in charge of all the stories. He was a damned good storyteller.

CHAPTER FOUR

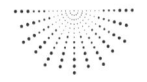

"Under no circumstances can you reveal that you are a true witch," Baba Yaga announced as she reeled off the rules for the Witchypoo Convention to Sassy and me. "No magic shall be performed in front of humans unless it's a life or death situation. You will behave and refrain from zapping humans *or* each other bald. The Goddess will be monitoring your progress and will blast your asses into next year if you screw up."

"You mean fuck up?" I asked with a yawn.

"You eat with that mouth?" Baba Yaga demanded with narrowed eyes.

"She most certainly fucking does," Sassy answered for me.

I almost laughed, but Baba was starting to sparkle ominously. Not a good sign.

Baba Yorudeass had shown up at seven am. Her outfit was so loud and garish I almost slugged her. Henry and Audrey had taken such a long nap yesterday that they decided to stay up most of the night. While I was thankful that I'd enjoyed multiple orgasms yesterday afternoon, I was exhausted today. Staring at a bossy-ass witch clad in yellow spandex dotted with purple feathers and sequins at the butt crack of dawn wasn't working for me.

"And what exactly am I supposed to do if everyone starts pooping?" Sassy demanded, staring daggers at anyone brave enough to make eye contact with her.

"No one will be *pooping*," Baba Yaga snapped and rolled her eyes. "We have already established that."

"Oh yeah. Right," Sassy said with her own eye roll. "They're all going to hold it. Which is waaaaay unhealthy."

My idiotic BFF was treading on some thin ice smack-talking our fashion-impaired leader, but she didn't seem to be concerned. I was actually kind of proud of Sassy the same way a parent would be if she'd learned her child had head-butted the school bully. Not that violence was ever the way to go, but sometimes it was appropriate… or at least satisfying… or funny.

Sassy wasn't a morning person at all. She was grumpy about being yanked out of bed by Marge and poofed over to my house against her will. She'd already blown up my coffee table, the TV and two lamps. Possibly because I was basically asleep on my feet or maybe it was because I was pissed that my shit was being destroyed, but I'd already zapped Sassy bald. Of course, I felt bad and gave her back her hair as soon as I woke up a bit, but not until she threatened to decrease my bust size. I really liked my boobs.

"I need to eat or I'm going to throat punch someone," Sassy muttered.

"No worries," Marge sang, sounding far too bright and cheery for the early hour. "Jeeves, Fabio, Roy, Mac, and the babies are creating a breakfast feast as we speak."

"Goddess in crotch-less panties, that could certainly turn out to be a shitshow," I groaned, wondering if I was going to have to magically repair my kitchen. Mac, Jeeves and my dad, Fabio were excellent cooks. My children were amazingly destructive in the kitchen. And Roy? Roy Bermangoggleshitz couldn't cook to save his formerly evil life.

Roy was a newly reformed assface of a warlock. He was Sassy's dad and Marge's one and only true love. I'd gone from wanting to enhance his looks with a thousand warts to loving him like one would love a seriously dysfunctional drunk uncle —the kind of guy who tells off-color jokes and burps at the dinner table and doesn't say excuse me. However, he'd basically given his life for the lives of Henry and Audrey. Thanks to the Goddess and Marge's magical kiss, he was alive and kicking. But he still couldn't cook.

"Moving on," Baba Yaga said, shaking her head. "As I told you, we're not sure what the problem is. We just have a feeling there's a problem."

"That's about as clear as mud," I muttered as I opened the front door and ushered everyone outside. If Sassy was going to blow shit up, it was going to be in my yard, not my house.

"Don't make me flip my witch switch," Baba Yaga warned as she flounced out of the house with Marge on her heels.

"I wanna drop a house on her," Sassy whispered as she slowly dragged her ass outside.

I bit back my laugh and followed the group of grumpy witches. I didn't want to go to the Witchypoo Convention, but if it meant getting a break from Baba Yobutthole, the trip was beginning to appeal.

"So let me get this straight," I said as I led the crabby posse a safe distance from my house. "We're supposed to find some assmonkey witches who are involved in *shenanigans*—whatever the hell *that* means—and we can't use magic to stop them."

"Is shenanigans a Canadian word?" Sassy asked, shielding her eyes against the sun.

Without missing a beat, Marge nodded so Sassy wouldn't get perturbed and uproot a bunch of trees. And speaking of trees... Sleepy, Doc, Sneezy, Grumpy and Sponge Bob had meandered over, tearing the yard to shreds. Mac was getting seriously annoyed with my giant wooden minions, but luckily he was mated to a fabu witch that could repair the damage. Sadly, there was a lot of damage.

"Can you fuckers be a little less destructive?" I demanded, crossing my arms over my chest and glaring at them.

"*Would that make you happy, O Hangry One?*" Sponge Bob inquired, perplexed.

No one could hear the trees talk except me. However, I was pretty sure Henry and Audrey understood them as well.

"Duh," I snapped with an eye roll. "I'm the Shifter Wanker, not a landscaper. And what the heck does hangry mean?"

"Hungry and pissed," Sassy volunteered since she, Marge and Baba Yaga could hear my side of the conversation. "It's a German word or possibly Canadian. I'm definitely hangry right now."

Well, Sponge Bob had gotten the hangry part right. Sassy and the origin of the word? Not so much.

"*As you wish,*" Sneezy said, bowing to me.

It was all kinds of weird to see a tree bow to you. I kept thinking they might snap in half. So far so good. They were still in one enormous piece.

In a flash of lightning, the yard was repaired. I narrowed my eyes at the dummies and tried not to laugh. "You mean to tell me that you never needed to uproot the ground to move?"

"*Nope,*" Doc told me.

All five of my leaf-covered dorkos chuckled and rocked back and forth in the morning breeze. At least they hadn't started in with the horrible tree jokes.

"*Zelda! What did the tree do when the bank closed?*" Grumpy asked with a high-pitched giggle. He was the happiest of the trees despite his name.

I stood corrected. This could take a while if I didn't play

along. "I have no clue and you guys can only ask three riddles. You feel me?"

"*It started its own branch,*" Grumpy announced as he wiggled with glee and a ton of his leaves fell to the ground almost burying a shocked Baba Yaga.

My evil smirk grew wide. "You guys can do ten more."

"*What type of tree fits in your hand?*" Sponge Bob shouted, shaking with excitement and further covering a now annoyed Baba Yaga.

"I don't know," I replied, lying. They'd told this one practically every day since they'd shown up.

"*A palm tree!*"

"*How did the warlock get hurt while raking leaves?*" Sleepy asked, not wanting to be left out.

"How?" I asked.

"*The warlock fell out of the tree!*" Sleepy screeched with delight, not sleepy at all.

Leaves exploded from his branches and Baba Yaga disappeared for the most part. It was all kinds of awesome... and then not.

"*Enough,*" Baba Yaga roared, shooting out of the leaf pile like a pissed off bullet.

Not only was she irate, she was glowing like a freakin' firework.

"Look out, people. I think she's hangry," Sassy pointed out with a grin.

Floating back down to solid ground, Baba waved her hands and scattered the massive leaf pile she'd been under.

"Are your trees done with riddle time?" she asked so calmly I blanched.

"Yep. Done," I promised.

"Good," she snapped, not realizing her overly lacquered hair-do was covered in leaves. I wasn't about to tell her. She was still glowing and I valued my life. "However, they're here for a reason—and it's *not* to bury me alive. Did they bother to tell you that?"

"Umm… nope," I said, glancing over at my wooden boys. "What were you actually supposed to tell me, dudes?"

"*Not tell*," Grumpy explained. "*Give*."

"Okay, I'll bite. What are you supposed to give me?"

Sleepy shuddered and I heard him crack in a few places. A fragrant pine scented wind began to blow and shimmering dark green crystals floated through the branches of my minions. The sun shone brighter and my trees stood taller. It was majestically enchanting.

Aside from the bad jokes and the yard destruction, they were actually pretty dang cool to have as minions. They were far more pleasant than Baba Yaga's minions — a grumpy group of bobble-headed warlock douchebags.

As the wind picked up and tossed the long wild grasses around, I was sure I heard a beautiful melody on the breeze. With a grunt and a giggle, Sleepy trembled and swayed. A thin, short stick of wood popped out from his leafy branches and made figure eights in the air as it found its way to me. It landed at my feet in a small bed of green crystals. It was alive—or it seemed to be.

"*For you, O Hangry and Lovely One. With this wand of sorts, you can summon others like us from anywhere in the world*," Doc explained.

"Dude, seriously? I can call trees to me that aren't mine?" I asked as I reverently and warily picked up the stick.

"All trees are yours, Zelda," Marge said, bowing in respect to my minions. "You have the power to summon all living trees."

"However, I'd suggest you take this gift and use it with *extreme* caution," Baba Yaga told me as she admired my simple yet wildly powerful stick.

"Do I get one too?" Sassy asked, finally waking up.

"No, my dear," Marge said, gently touching Sassy's cheek. "Your gifts are very different from Zelda's. I will be giving you a bottle of the magic balancing potion to use in the case of an emergency."

I ran my hands through my hair and squeezed my eyes shut for a brief moment. I wanted to say a whole bunch of really bad words strung together, but figured that wouldn't really go over well. If the Goddess was watching—and I was pretty sure she was—I'd get an ass zapping like no other if I was rude about such a monumental gift. However, I still had to let it rip.

Roger, my dumbass therapist, told me holding my feelings in was not smart. Smart wasn't the first word that came to mind when describing me, but I definitely wasn't going to hold it in.

"Soooooo, this is kind of large. You know, finding out I can *uproot the fucking world* if I'm in the mood. Is there a good reason why you people are saddling me with this shit? I'm not exactly the most responsible witch we know."

"The Goddess allows everything to happen when it's supposed to," Baba Yaga said with a smile.

"If that's true, then am I to believe I'm gonna *need* this stick?" I asked, pressing the bridge of my nose in frustration. *Shenanigans* were turning out to be very bad indeed.

"I hope not," Marge said, reaching into her Chanel bag and pulling out two little palm-sized machines. "These are walkie-talkies. Since magic is prohibited unless the circumstances are dire, you can use these to communicate with each other at the Witchypoo Convention."

"Ohhhhhhhh, for real?" Sassy asked, hopping up and down with excitement. "I've always wanted a walkie-talkie. We never got any of the cool stuff at the orphanage." She paused and deflated for a moment. "We never got anything at the orphanage."

Now that I had my own children, thinking about Sassy being dumped at an orphanage for witches when she was a little girl made me ill. How could a mother do that to her child? Although I hadn't fared much better and I hadn't been dumped. Nope, my mother had tried to kill me—a fact that still gave me nightmares occasionally.

"Speaking of mothers," I started.

"We weren't," Baba Yaga pointed out correctly.

"Okay. Fine," I agreed with an eye roll. "But where exactly is my mother now?"

Carol and Marge exchanged loaded glances and my stomach tightened. Was my sorry excuse for a mother on the loose? She didn't possess magic anymore, so she couldn't harm anyone. Although, there were many ways to harm even without magic.

"She's in the pokey in Salem," Baba Yaga said. "Why do you ask? Has she tried to communicate with you?"

I shuddered and then sighed. "No. Not at all. I was just wondering."

"Does she have to wear a skanky orange jumpsuit like we did?" Sassy inquired, scrunching her nose in disgust.

That was another thing that gave me nightmares. The orange fucking jumpsuit had clashed hideously with my red hair. The pain of being incarcerated in the pokey had almost been outweighed by the gag-inducing prison wear.

Marge nodded, still staring at me strangely. "What made you bring your mother up?"

Shrugging, I sighed. Honestly, Carol aka Baba Yopaininmyass was more of a mother to me than my mother had ever been. Baba said what she meant, had rules that she stuck to, and she loved me. I'd never admitted it—and probably never would—but I loved her too. The fact that she and my dad were shacking up and in luuurve made me secretly happy, as much as it gave me gas.

"I suppose it was thinking about Sassy in the orphanage

and then thinking about my own babies," I told Marge. "It still boggles my mind that a mother wouldn't love her child."

Baba Yaga smiled sadly and took my hand in hers. She and Marge were no strangers to awful mothers themselves. Endora —their pathetic excuse for an egg donor—had recently tried to steal my children, kill me and rule the magical world. Endora was *not* in the magical pokey. Nope. She was far too dangerous. The mother of the two most powerful witches in existence was residing with the Goddess at the moment. I was quite sure it was not even a little bit pleasant after what Endora had done. The Goddess did not fuck around when it came to punishment.

"Sometimes the world doesn't work in natural order. Sometimes the fairy tales we dream are not the ones we live," Baba Yaga said quietly.

"However," Marge continued, putting her arm around her sister. "We are not slaves to our beginnings, Zelda, unless we choose that option. At some point we are given a choice—a path, so to speak. Whether we elect to go in a new direction and leave the past behind us is completely up to us."

"That's pretty deep for seven thirty in the butt crack of the morning," I said, smiling at Marge and Baba.

"I'm good like that," Marge replied with a wink.

What she said calmed me. I had chosen a new path, but I wasn't stupid or arrogant enough to think I'd done it on my own. Baba Yaga and the Goddess had watched over me. As much as I had and would continue to give Baba Yaga crap, I owed her a buttload.

Sassy raised her hand and waited patiently to be called on.

"Yes, Sassy?" Baba Yaga asked, looking a little scared.

Since we never knew what would come out of Sassy's mouth, Baba had every right to be a bit frightened.

"I'm still hangry. What else do we need to know?"

With a giant sigh of relief, Baba nodded her head and got back to business. "The Witchypoo Convention is in Lexington,

Kentucky. We've made hotel reservations for you and your mates next door to the convention center. It occurs over three days starting tomorrow. The festivities are held in a place called Rupp Arena."

"Well, that certainly makes sense," Sassy said with a grunt of laughter.

"Not following why that's funny," I said, cocking my head to the side and trying to figure out what was going on inside Sassy's whacky brain.

"*Rump* Arena is a great name for a poop convention. You know, since poop comes out of the rump," she explained.

"Good Goddess," Baba Yaga groaned and let her chin drop to her chest. "*Rupp* Arena. Not *Rump* Arena."

"Whoops. My bad," Sassy replied with a giggle. "Can we eat now?"

"Yes, Sassy. We can," Baba Yaga said with a laugh. "And one more thing. You can use your magic, but use it wisely and carefully."

"Roger that," Sassy yelled as she took to the air.

Sassy literally flew back to the house. We didn't need brooms to fly even though Sassy was a big fan of using one. I'd tried it once and crash-landed right in the middle of Main Street in front of all the good folk of Assjacket. I was not going to make that embarrassing mistake again.

Marge followed Sassy up to the house, which left Carol and me alone.

"Would you like to talk about your mother anymore?" she asked with concern.

I glanced over at Baba Yaga and grinned. She was a hot mess—covered in leaves and glittering spandex. I couldn't adore her more.

"You promise not to repeat what I say?" I questioned her.

"Witch's Honor that anything you say will never leave my lips."

I didn't even have to think about it—which shocked me. But I had taken my own path. My past didn't define me thanks to the horribly dressed witch who cared about me.

"I love you," I told her.

Baba Yaga's eyes grew wide and she quickly swiped at a tear. Her smile made her beauty so incredible I almost had to look away. "And I love you," she replied softly.

I took her hand in mine and started off to the house. I was hangry too.

"If you tell anyone, I'll totally deny it," I warned her.

"I promise to keep your dastardly secret, Zelda," she said, squeezing my hand.

Of course, it wasn't really a secret at all. Even though my mom hadn't loved me, I was able to love others.

And I did love Baba Yaga.

However, I still didn't want her damn job.

CHAPTER FIVE

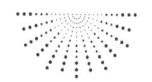

"You do realize you have more syrup on your plate than your children do," my dad, Fabio informed me with a grin and a raised brow.

He sat across from me at our large kitchen table as I shoveled delicious pancakes into my mouth. His chin rested on his hand and he watched me in fascination. My dad's face was so much like mine it was a little freaky. It was like looking into a mirror and staring at what I would look like as a man. Of course, he was hundreds of years old and I wasn't, but that didn't matter. Since all magical beings stopped aging around thirty-ish, we really did look like twins. But as much as I loved him, maple syrup was serious business and I was a hangry witch. He was not going to fuck with my sugar intake.

I flipped Fabio off covertly so my kids wouldn't see me. Henry had already told everyone in the room they were sexy, much to my horror. I didn't need my son lifting his birdie finger in greeting. My dad's belly laugh warmed me all over. We'd started our relationship off on a weird foot. He was my cat and I ran over him three times with my car. Not exactly a stellar beginning—I spent nine months in the pokey for that little *mishap*.

The simple truth was we would always be weird, but we were perfect for each other and I adored him. Plus he had fabu taste in designer clothes and seriously enjoyed shopping for me. I was eighty-five percent sure he paid for most of it. He was loaded, thanks to his gambling habit, but still had extremely sticky fingers. Having Fabio in my life now almost made up for being raised by my mother. Of course, he'd taught the twins to play poker, but certain things about a person would never change. My dad lived right on the edge of being legal.

"Your point, Fabdudio?" I asked, aiming my fork at his forehead.

"No point, just an observation," he replied, wiggling his fingers and turning my fork into a flower.

Reaching across the table, I pilfered his fork and went back to my pancake pile. Thank the Goddess, witches had an insanely fast metabolism. I'd eaten a house while I was pregnant—granted it was a cookie house, but a *house*—and I still looked fantastic.

Clearing his throat dramatically, Bermangoggleshitz stood up and took the floor. It made me a little itchy. Sassy and I were still occasionally training with her dad to control our dark magic. If he was going to suggest a session before we left, I was going to zap him hairless. However, that wasn't what he wanted to share. Nope. It was far more horrifying than that.

"I'd like everyone to know that *I made the pancakes*," Bermangoggleshitz announced grandly as he bowed and kissed a wildly alarmed Marge on the top her head.

Marge quickly and subtly pushed her plate of pancakes away... as did Baba Yaga and Sassy.

I almost puked in my mouth. I was now terrified that I'd been poisoned. Roy was a worse cook than I was and I burned water.

"We threw his batch out," Fabio whispered to me with a slight gag. "They resembled charred hockey pucks with hair."

I sighed very audibly and let my forehead fall to the table in relief. The thud was loud. Thankfully, Roy didn't seem to notice—he was far too proud of himself. At least my kitchen was still standing. I was shocked that Roy had been allowed to cook at all. The warlock was trying really hard to fit in here in Assjacket and we all wanted him to feel welcome. However, burnt hairy pancakes would have sent me over the edge. It would be a shame if Roy left my house with enormous knockers and fifty warts on his handsome face.

"Alrighty then," Mac said, seating himself next to me and handing me a fresh plate of pancakes. He was totally getting a blowjob later for that. "We'll be gone for three days. I trust that Henry and Audrey will be well looked after."

"I will kill the shit out of anything evil that comes near them," Roy promised, crossing his heart.

"Shit," Henry shouted with a delighted squeal.

"Sexy shit," Audrey added, not to be outdone by her profane brother.

Roy paled considerably and slapped his hand over his mouth. "Sorry," he whispered between splayed fingers. "My bad."

Waving his hand, Fabio magically duct taped Roy's mouth shut. Amazingly Roy did nothing in retaliation. The two warlocks usually liked to best each other with violent results, but Roy knew he was in the doghouse at the moment. The protection of my children was one of the things Roy took very seriously. Along with Sassy and Marge, my babies were his world. He'd promised the Goddess he would always keep them safe until his last breath.

I believed that. However, I was doing a fine job of enhancing my children's potty vocabulary on my own. I didn't need any help from Roy Bermangoggleshitz.

"Not only will my grandchildren be protected by Marge, Roy, Carol and me—all the Shifters in Assjacket have volunteered to have play dates here at the house," Fabio said, pulling a sleepy Audrey onto his lap.

My babies should be exhausted considering they made each and every one of their stuffed animals fly around their room all night. They had a lot of stuffed animals, thanks to my dad and Baba Yaga. Even though keeping my eyes open was kind of difficult, last night had been perfect in every way. We all rode on Mac's wolf and then we watched *Monsters Inc.* twice—or *Monster Inky* as Henry called it. Audrey had plans to marry Mike Wazowski when she grew up. Henry's first crush was *Elastigirl*. Interesting choices, but my little ones were very interesting people.

"Some noodles need a nap," I said with a grin as Henry laid his head on top of his syrupy pancakes. "And possibly a bath…"

"Ohhhhh, can I give them their bath?" Sassy asked with her hands clasped together.

"I'll help," Jeeves volunteered quickly with a loving smile to Sassy. "That way we won't flood the house."

"That is so hot and sweet and hot," Sassy told Jeeves as she slapped him on the bottom. "Our chipmunks like to bathe in the pond, so I don't get to do bath time at our house. And considering the gnarly little bastards are old enough to be my grandfathers, that would be all kinds of weird. I've told them to tell people that they're twelve so no one thinks I'm old."

"Umm… okay," I said, squinting at my BFF and her kangaroo Shifter mate—who was also Mac's adopted son, making me Sassy's mother-in-law. Terrifying but true. She was forbidden to call me Mom. She'd tried once and it didn't end well for her. Suffice it to say she likes being a woman more than a man. "Just make sure that Audrey doesn't conjure up a hurricane and Henry doesn't add an octopus to the tub. Bath time yesterday was a shitshow."

"Shitshow," Audrey agreed.

"Do I need to duct tape your mouth too?" Fabio inquired with a grin.

I looked up at the ceiling and groaned. "Probably."

"No octopus and no hurricanes! Buuut, did you know that octopuses have three hearts and blue blood—not because they're rich or anything. It's just blue. Kinda gross if you ask me," Sassy told a fascinated Henry and Audrey as she and Jeeves scooped up the twins and headed out of the kitchen. "And those slimy swimmers also have nine freakin' brains! My guess is that they can totally speak Canadian."

"Is that true?" Mac asked, confused.

"That octopuses speak Canadian?" I asked with a laugh.

Mac grinned and shook his head. "Umm… no. The rest of it."

"I'd hazard a guess that the answer is yes. Sassy is obsessed with Animal Planet."

"We'll go get story time ready," Marge said as she took Roy's hand and led him out of the kitchen. "We'll also monitor bath time."

"Thank you," I said, relieved. Sassy meant well, but tended to get over excited and blow shit up. My living room furniture was proof.

Fabio held out his hand to me and smiled. "Zelda, come take a walk with me."

"Why? Am I in trouble?" I asked, eyeing him warily.

"Did you do anything bad?" he inquired.

"Define bad," I shot back.

My dad shook his head and chuckled. "Come on."

"Go," Baba Yaga said, shooing us out of the kitchen. "Mac and I will clean up."

I glanced over my shoulder at a terrified Mac. Being alone

with Baba Yaga could do that to a person—even an alpha werewolf. I loved her, but she was still a scary motherhumper.

"You be nice to Mac," I told her as my dad pushed me out the front door.

"Define nice," she replied with an evil little giggle.

"Oh shit," was the last thing I heard Mac say before Fabio shoved me out of the house.

"Where are we going?" I asked my dad as I followed him down the stairs of the front porch.

"To town," he replied.

"Why?"

"I want to show you something."

And with a snap of his fingers, we poofed to town.

CHAPTER SIX

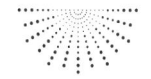

Our town, if you could call it that, consisted of Main Street. The town square was dominated by a cement statue of a bear missing one side of its head. The rest of the block included a barbershop, hardware store, gas station, diner, a few other rundown buildings, and a mom and pop grocery store.

It was a total dump and that suited the Shifters of Assjacket just fine. Humans drove right through the dilapidated town without a backward glance. Inside the ramshackle structures, everything was pure enchantment. Everything from the Assjacket Diner to my idiot therapist Roger the rabbit's office was charming and lovely behind the broken down exteriors. The town was a massive sleight of hand, so to speak. It was a testament to the brilliance of my friends since the Shifters and witches lived very public yet secret lives.

"Soooo," Fabio said, bouncing on his feet in excitement. "I bought a building in town."

"Define bought," I said, narrowing my eyes at my dad.

"Not following," he replied in a vague tone, not making eye contact.

Trying not to grin, I groaned instead. "Did you pay actual money for this building?"

"Basically."

"That's a non-answer," I told him. "Did you *procure* this building?"

Fabio became quite fascinated with the half-headed cement bear. "If you're implying that I *stole* it, I didn't."

"Okay, that's a good start," I said, wondering where everyone was. It was a lovely day and no one was out. "Did you sucker someone?"

"You're getting warmer."

"Would a poker game happen to have been involved?" I pressed.

"Very hot," he replied sheepishly.

I shook my head and sighed. "Dad, did you cheat in the game?"

"Burning hot," he admitted.

A leopard couldn't change his spots and a warlock couldn't change… much. I knew Fabio was trying really hard. I also knew that millions of his questionably gained funds went to charity. My dad was a very good kind of bad-ish dude.

"Who used to own this building?"

"Bob the beaver," Fabio said. "Word around town was that he had plans to turn it into a large dam."

"For real?" I asked, surprised. Bob was an odd one. He had a unibrow that should be illegal and had a habit of eating berries that gave him gas, but building a massive dam on Main Street? That could be a freakin' mess if it broke.

"Absolutely," Fabio said, clearly relieved to be telling the truth if his direct eye contact was anything to go by. "And Bob was happy to get rid of it—lots of plumbing problems—hence his idea to turn it into a dam. Roger the rabbit was horrified as his place of business is right next door. He was my second in the game."

"My therapist cheated at cards?" I demanded, tucking that little nugget away for blackmail purposes if the rabbit tried to get me to use interpretive dance to express my feelings ever again.

"Umm... no?" Fabio whispered, realizing he'd outed the nose twitcher. "But if it would please you, I would be happy to pay actual money to Bob."

"It would," I told him with a smile. "And you'll feel better too."

"Umm... I wasn't actually feeling bad, but making you happy makes me happy, and that's why I bought the building."

"Okay, thank you. But I don't really need a building, dad. I have an office to heal the clumsy ass Shifters on my own property."

"This is true," Fabio said, smiling. "However, Assjacket is missing something very important."

"It is?"

"It is," he confirmed, leading me over to a crumbling bench and seating me.

He was nervous. Now I was itchy. My dad's ideas could result in prison time. We'd just found each other. I didn't want him to end up in the pokey.

"Zelda," he said, shoving his hands in his pockets and pacing in circles. "I wasn't there for you as a child. I missed so much that we can never get back. I know we have the future, but I live with so much regret and guilt. It sickens me when I think about that woman raising you."

"Fabdudio, you didn't know about me," I told him, pulling him down on the bench next to me. He was making me dizzy with the pacing. "I'm not mad or upset or anything. I love you and I'm just fucking delighted that we're together now. And my past is just that—*past*. It doesn't define me. I'm proud to be a somewhat materialistic, Shifter healing, profane mother."

"You're a wonderful mother," he said with pride.

"They're toddlers," I reminded him. "That remains to be seen."

"You love them?" my dad questioned.

"Yep. I would die for them."

"As I would for you," he said and then smiled sadly. "I didn't get to go on field trips with you or any Father-Daughter dances. We didn't have magic class with each other like a father and daughter should. I didn't get to teach you how to play blackjack or take you to dance lessons. And I know I can't make up for lost time, so…"

"So you bought me a building instead?" I asked, a little confused.

Fabio nodded and grinned. "Follow me."

The front of the building looked just like every other façade in Assjacket—awful. However, the inside? The inside made me cry.

"It's for you and Henry and Audrey and all the children of Assjacket," Fabio whispered as he gently wiped the tears from my eyes.

It was a school. A lovely school with state-of-the-art technology. I wasn't about to ask how he'd amassed so many machines. It wasn't the right time. It was filled with books and games and little desks. It was warm and inviting and perfect.

And I now knew where everyone had been hiding. Wanda the raccoon was here with her son Bo and her mate Kurt. DeeDee, the deer who owned the Assjacket Diner with Wanda was grinning broadly and waving. My buddy Simon the skunk was playing with the small instruments and having a ball. Bob the beaver was straightening up the small library and nodding with satisfaction. Roger, my rabbit therapist, was leading a line of little ones around to check out all the computers and games. And at the front of the line of children were a spiffily cleaned up and giggling Henry and Audrey.

In fact, all my peeps were here. Mac, Baba Yaga, Marge, Roy,

Sassy and Jeeves. Clearly, I was the only one who didn't know about the surprise. They had to have left right after Fabio and I did... very sneaky. But that was just fine with me. I adored surprises—especially ones like this.

Fabio clapped his hands and got everyone's attention. "Welcome to the Assjacket School, my friends. You are standing in the Zelda Building—named after my beautiful daughter. As time goes on, and we need to expand, we shall."

"I have two more buildings I don't want," Bob announced with his unibrow waggling. "I'd be up for a round or two of blackjack."

"I'll take that under consideration," Fabio said with a grin. "However, to celebrate the grand opening we are going to have a Father-Daughter Dance."

"Now?" I asked with a giggle.

"Now," Fabio said.

Simon pulled out his guitar and a few of his skunk buddies joined him on drums and a keyboard. Baba Yaga snapped her fingers and a motorized mirror ball appeared on the ceiling—straight out of the eighties. It was all kinds of cheesy and all kinds of great.

As the music started Fabio bowed to me. "May I have this dance, daughter?"

I almost couldn't speak it was so sweet, but he was expecting an answer. "Yes, you may, father," I told him as I placed my hand in his.

Fabio was a great dancer. Me? Not at all, but it didn't matter. My dad held me in his arms and whirled me around the beautiful school that he'd named for me. Out of the corner of my eye, I saw Roy lead Sassy out for a dance. She was crying and I was pretty sure Roy was too. On the flip side of that Mac and Audrey were all smiles. Mac held our daughter in his arms and swayed to the music. And just so Henry wouldn't feel left out, Baba Yaga flew him to the dance area and cut the rug with my little dude.

It was so beautifully overwhelming I almost couldn't breathe.

"Thank you, dad."

"You're welcome, Zelda," he whispered and kissed the top of my head.

We couldn't make up for the lost years, but this might just be the medicine to heal all the old wounds.

CHAPTER SEVEN

"Are weese dere yet?" Fat Bastard asked for the fiftieth time in the last hour.

At least this time, he'd raised his head out from between his legs to speak. The last four inquiries had been punctuated with slurps.

We really should have just poofed to Lexington, Kentucky, but Baba Yaga had insisted we drive like normal humans. So Mac, Sassy, Jeeves, my cats, and I were all packed into the car. It was *awesome*… not. As far as I was concerned, normal was seriously overrated. My crotch goblins were driving everyone nuts.

"You fond of your nads?" I asked Fat Bastard.

"Youse knows I am, dollface," he said making a little kitty thumbs up with his furry paw.

Fat Bastard, Jango Fett and Boba Fett were mine for better or worse—most of the time it was *worse*. They were rotund, fur covered, smack-talking buttholes. They were also my familiars. Yessssssss, I loved them but the cats were gross. Their obsessive testes cleansing was at the very top of the Yuck List.

"Then I'd suggest you keep them out of your mouth for the

remainder of the trip, which is a half an hour. You feel me?" I asked, eyeing my corpulent cat.

"I feel youse," Fat Bastard said with a grunt of laughter.

"Nows, I did hear dat the Bastard can't canoodle wid his cockbeans, but was youse just talkin' to the Bastard, or does dat go for me and Jango too?" Boba Fett inquired politely, his back leg perched high over his head.

"If you want to keep your wrinkled crotch purses, then it goes for all three of you," I answered just as politely. However, I was deadly serious.

"Would youse *really* remove the nickel ticklers?" Jango asked, covering his tiny balls just in case I used his as an example.

"Oh, my Goddess," I shouted on a laugh. "How many names do you have for your nuts?"

"Oh, shit," I heard Mac say under his breath as he stepped on the gas to get us there faster. "You've done it now, Zelda."

Mac was correct and sadly we would all have to pay for my horrifying mistake.

"Well now, dats a subject close to my heart," Fat Bastard announced, hopping up into the front seat and landing his huge kitty ass in my lap. "Deres meat clackers and man berries."

"Don't youse forget ball-slaw and badoodles," Jango chimed in.

"Youse mangy motherfuckers left out magic flesh grapes and double bubbles," Boba added.

"I'm going to hurl," I muttered, knowing I was fully to blame for this lesson in nicknames for scrotum.

For the next twenty-three minutes, we learned over five hundred ways to describe balls.

Mac, Sassy, Jeeves, and I were now officially scarred for life.

"Jeeves and I will go check in with the local Shifter pack," Mac said as he pulled me in for a quick hug. We'd checked into our rooms then went back to the car to speak in complete privacy. Mac had found a great spot on the street right across from Rupp Arena. "Don't hesitate to call if anything goes wrong in the venue. We'll meet back at the hotel in three hours. If someone doesn't show, call in backup."

"Got it," I said, checking for my walkie-talkie.

Marge had provided two more for Mac and Jeeves. And they weren't normal walkie-talkies. Nope, these were infused with enchantment. The range of communication was over fifty miles and we were the only four that could use the private magical channel.

Rupp Arena was huge and the Witchypoo Convention had apparently taken over the entire place. Lexington was all kinds of charming with fountains and flowering trees everywhere, but I still preferred Assjacket.

"Jeeves, you be careful," Sassy said as she kissed him and then squished his cheeks. "There are apparently a lot of constipated people in this town. Crap could get bad."

"Sassy, you just made a really bad pun," I said, rolling my eyes.

"Well, if I did it was a shitty one because I didn't even know I did it," she replied looking confused.

I was tempted to explain but that could take days. We had shenanigans to find.

"We're out," Mac said as he and Jeeves got out of the car and walked down the street.

The local Shifter headquarters a few blocks away—it doubled as a veterinary clinic. Pretty clever.

"Sweet cheeks," Fat Bastard said as he waddled out of the car. "Are weese comin' with youse?"

"Yep," I said, locking up with a key. It was incredibly strange not to use magic since it was second nature, but Baba had made the rules very clear. No magic unless absolutely necessary. "And it would be great if you could pretend to be normal cats."

"So what youse is sayin' is dat we can't spray paint no profanities on dem walls?" Jango asked, pointing to the side of the convention center.

Breathing in through my nose and out through my mouth, I nodded. "Yes. That would be a big fucking no-no. That would be a wax you bald and time out in your kennel for a week no-no."

"Got it, Hot Potato," Fat Bastard said. "Howsevers, what are the ground rules if weese find some feline hookers? Is the wild thing off limits?"

"Are you fucking serious? There are *cat hookers*?" I snapped, wishing I'd left the fleshy, horny idiots at home.

"Jango was a gigolo for a decade back in the 1930's," Boba announced as Jango preened.

Jango Fett marched back and forth in front of us with his tail held high and his tubby belly dragging on the ground. It was all I could do not to laugh. If there ever really was a cat gigolo, Jango didn't exactly come to mind.

"I'm gonna pretend I didn't hear any of that shit," I said, giving them a look that made them zip it. "We are here to find some freakin' shenanigans. We are *working*. I have no clue who we're looking for or what we're doing here..."

"But it's *not* pooping," Sassy added, interrupting me. "You have to hold your poop until we get back to Assjacket. My guess is that there are no toilets in Rump Arena... or litter boxes."

"Rupp Arena," I corrected her. I wasn't even going to touch the bathroom thing.

"My bad," she said, holding her hands up. "I'd suggest a liquid diet while we're in town. Peeing in the parking lot is far more couth than dropping the kids off at the lake on Vine Street."

"Are you done?" I asked, pressing the bridge of my nose.

"I am," Sassy replied. "You can finish now. You were doing great. I just wanted to be clear about the poop thing."

This was going to be a really long three days. Hopefully, we could find the shenanigans in the first hour and put an end to it. Standing in for Baba Yaga and Cookie Witch was hard and we'd barely begun. I was so not taking this job.

"Okay," I said watching a line of horribly dressed fake witches file into the venue. "I believe I can safely say this is going to suck ass. Only use your power if you have to. When we get inside, we'll split up and case the joint."

"Hot Pants," Fat Bastard said with a wide kitty grin. "Youse is soundin' like a wise guy."

"Thank you. I think," I told the porcine dummy with a grin of my own. "I just want to say up front, I have no fucking clue what I'm doing. I have no plan. If we need one, I will yank it out of my ass and we'll wing it. Cool?"

"I'm in, dollface," Fat Bastard said. "And if weese sees a feline hooker, weese will walk right past."

"Weese will?" Jango asked, appalled.

"Let me amend," Fat Bastard corrected himself. "*After* weese give her our business card and flash our giggle berries, weese will walk on past."

"That was entirely too fucking much information," I said, shaking my head and wanting to zap them. However, I was smarter than that.

Any magic shot at my crotch goblins came right back at the person who shot it. My fat, hairy ball lickers were the most amazing shields in the Goddess's Universe. But they were also gross.

"Just sniff around and see if you detect any real magic in the arena."

"Goddess in gauchos," Sassy squealed. "This is gonna be fun!"

"Fun isn't the word that comes to mind," I muttered, watching more faux witches, mummies and vampires enter the building. "But I can tell you this. We're dressed really wrong."

"Holy shit on a sharp stick," Sassy said with a laugh. "You're correct. Baba Yoleaveinformationout forgot to tell us to bring our Halloween costumes."

"She most certainly did," I grumbled. "You ready?"

"I was born ready, BFF."

That was the answer I wanted to hear, but it terrified me at the same time. Sassy and I were a good team, but she wasn't exactly stable. And since I wasn't either, it was anyone's guess how this was going to play out.

"Let's do this."

Walking across the street in our brightly colored designer dresses that made us stick out like a sore fucking thumb, we entered the Witchypoo Convention. My portly familiars were immediately drawn to a magician sawing a woman in half. Whatever. They'd catch up soon enough.

It was shenanigans time.

CHAPTER EIGHT

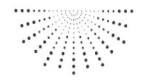

BACK AT THE WITCHYPOO CONVENTION...

DEALING WITH VERRUCA TROTCACKLER WHILE CHECKING IN HAD almost made me break my promise not to use magic. My cats had all but disappeared and Baba Yoidiot hadn't registered us. A teeny tiny bit of magic had been necessary. If Baba didn't like it, she could kiss my butt. At least I hadn't enhanced Verruca with warts—and she was asking for it. The asswipe had threatened to send us to the cauldron of eternal flame in Hell until we were fucking crispy, of all things.

If Verruca was anything like the freaks we were going to encounter, it would take an act of the Goddess to keep me from zapping every person dressed in a black robe and pointy hat.

The Witchypoo Convention was a hot mess... and *someone* was dealing in blood.

"Witches don't deal in blood, Verruca," I snapped. "Ever."

Verruca's eyes narrowed and she pursed her black lips unattractively. "How would *you* know? Someone dressed in Prada is not a *real* witch. I know a real witch when I see one."

Sassy grunted and raised her hands high in the air. Verruca was about to lose a body part—or gain one. I could never tell with Sassy. Shooting Sassy a look that made her reconsider barricading herself back under the table, she reluctantly let her hands fall to her sides.

Breathing in through my nose and slowly out through my mouth, I got up in Verruca's face. She was treading on some very thin ice. I took my fashion *very* seriously. "It's Stella McCartney. Not Prada. I only wear Prada on Tuesdays, Valencia Snotcracker."

"Ohhhh, good one," Sassy congratulated me.

"Thank you," I replied. "And Veronica... you should seriously get your eyes checked."

"Why?" she snapped.

"Because you clearly can't tell the difference between a real witch and a fake one."

On that note, we entered the sacred realm of Magical Mystery and Mayhem. It was a shitshow of epic proportions. There were enough counterfeit witches, vampires and mummies walking around to give me nightmares for the next century or two—but there was also real magic somewhere in the mass of ridiculousness.

Maybe there really was a reason to check this out. Or, maybe Baba Yaga was right out of her debatably sane mind. But then again, what the Hell did I expect? She did send us to the *Witchypoo Convention* at *Rump* Arena in *Hexington*, Kentucky...

Let the witch-hunt shenanigans begin.

"Oh. My. Goddess," Sassy gasped out, trembling from head to toe.

"What?" I hissed, frantically looking around for the illusive shenanigans that were freaking Sassy out. "What's wrong?"

"Brooms," she squealed. "They have an enormous broom display."

"Dude," I snapped, whacking her in the head. "Do *not* do that. I thought you found the fucking shenanigans."

"Sorry," she apologized. "My bad. At least it wasn't someone pooping."

Sassy's eyes were laser focused on the massive and ridiculous broom display. Fake witches were running around in a big circle with bushy sticks between their legs. I would have laughed if it wasn't so alarming. How in the Goddess's name did we get this kind of reputation? Witches were nothing like this.

"I want the blue one. It matches my eyes. I would look so hot zooming around on that," Sassy announced.

"Fine," I said, giving up. Sassy would be useless unless she got to see the brooms. "But don't even think about actually flying around the convention hall. There is no way to play that off as a magic trick. If you do, it will result in a permanent Mohawk. You feel me?"

"Yes!" Sassy squealed as she sprinted over to the brooms, knocking at least six mummies, two vampires and a magician over in her rabid excitement.

Since Sassy would be there for a while and my cats were probably now searching for feline floozies, that left me to actually do what we were supposed to do. Of course, I had no idea what that was, but I was going to do it anyway. I decided to just take a stroll around and see if I could find the real magic at the assbaggery event.

It was like one cavernous indoor garage sale of "magic" crap. The irony was that true magic didn't need any props—no brooms, no wands. Magic came from the Goddess and the earth she created. Real magic was everywhere. You just had to believe.

Even humans had their own special kind of magic—not at all like what I had—but many had a true connection with nature and spirituality. There was none of that here. Movies and TV had created the shitshow I was wandering through.

Booths lined the thirty or so aisles with charlatans hawking their wares. Although I was tempted to buy the t-shirt that read *If the Broom Fits… Ride It* for Sassy, I passed. The vials of potions were hilarious. I bought three for Baba Yaga and three for Marge… and then I caved and bought the damn broom t-shirt for Sassy. The attendees were taking themselves faaaar too seriously as they pushed and shoved to get to the latest in shitty witch-wear. There were chanting lessons, tables full of crystals and even a custom pointy hat booth.

I may or may not have caused the hat display to cave in on itself…

I was literally ignored because of my Stella McCartney dress. That was fine by me. Little did the black lipstick-wearing weirdos know that there were a few *real* witches in the building… or at least two of us. The egotistical side of me wanted to whip up a windstorm and scare the pointy black hats off the fake idiots, but that would be a bad thing. I knew it was a bad thing… a really bad thing.

But Goddess, I still wanted to do it.

Nope. Not gonna do it. I was mature. I was a mom. I healed Shifters, witches, and even my crotch goblins when they needed a tune-up.

I was above petty destructive violence even if it felt good sometimes to let it rip. However, I had no intention of going back to the pokey. Nine months for mowing down my cat slash dad with my car was enough for me. Thank the Goddess he had nine lives.

My fingers itched to do just a little something. But there was no reason to blow my cover. If there were shenanigans here, I needed to stay focused and find them.

And then the Goddess stepped in. Well, *maybe not*, but what happened was entirely out of my control… for the most part.

Verruca sauntered by with her posse of nerds dressed in black polyester robes and *laughed* at me. No one in a shitty Party City witch costume that called herself Trotcackler was allowed to laugh at me. Ever.

"Her last name is *Houstonordallas*. Can you believe that?" Verruca asked her freak brigade as they all laughed and pointed. "She thinks she's a *real* witch. Have you ever heard anything so stupid? We're the real deal. That hot mess is a pretender."

"Loser with a capital L," one of Verruca's buddies announced in her outdoor voice while making an L with her fingers and positioning it on her forehead.

My mouth twisted at the irony. Goddess in Spanx, high school wasn't even this bad.

They formed a tight clump and chanted something that sounded like a stuck pig in agony. Waving bottles of what I assumed was eye of newt but looked more like cricket turds, they proceeded to cast a *spell*. If I wasn't mistaken… *and I wasn't*… it was a spell aimed at me.

Of course, Verruca—the *most powerful spell caster in Hexington*—took the lead. I expected no less. Closing her eyes and doing a jig that made her look like she had to pee, she raised her wand high as her dorky minions dropped to their knees and began to chant in front of her. The milling vamps and mummies stopped their shopping to watch.

"Bubble, bubble, toil and trouble," Verruca grunted, swaying her hips and summoning her inner stripper.

"She thinks she's a witch
But she's only a double.
Out with the one who makes us sicken…
Only real witches here, not some fashionable chicken."

The mummies applauded and the vamps wandered off,

clearly bored with Verruca's gyrating sideshow. I had to hand it to her—at least it rhymed.

"I find a couple of profanities helps my spells," I informed the flabbergasted quartet who were either shocked I hadn't turned into a chicken yet, or they'd never been called out on the rug for crappy spell procedure. "It didn't exactly suck, but you could use some work, Verruca Hotcanker."

"Verruca *Trotcackler* is a spell goddess," a short, squat one sneered. "You should kiss the ground she walks on, skank."

"How does riffraff like that even get in?" a tall, gawky one demanded. "I say we kick her out."

Done. I was done.

Baba Yaga was going to owe me big for dealing with this shit. I was beginning to think her and Marge's lack of attendance had nothing to do with getting recognized by any real witches creating shenanigans. Sassy and I had been punked.

The rules that Baba Yoashtonkutcher had put in place were now moot. There was only so much a *real* witch could take. Plus they'd cast a bogus spell on me. As far as I was concerned, this was now a tit for tat situation.

"Wicked chickens lay deviled eggs," I said as I waved to the now confused group. The wave was sheer brilliance on my part. It looked like a social greeting... it was anything but.

"Say what?" Verruca asked, pointing her wand at me.

"Nothing at all, Verruca Squatcrapper," I shot back with a smile.

It was all kinds of awesome when the foursome began to lay eggs—dozens of brightly colored eggs. The vamps were interested again. The pointy-hatted buttholes were now in unladylike squats on the floor feeling like the chicken they'd stupidly tried to turn me into. Verruca's spell had backfired into an omelet machine. A few magicians circled the shrieking quartet and tried to figure out how they were doing it. Again, I may or may not have been responsible. Walking away quickly, I was grinning from ear to ear.

And then I wasn't.

The shot was discreet. The shot was precise. The shot hurt like a motherfucker. Holding back a stream of profanities took super witchy effort. I just hoped there wasn't a large burn hole in the butt of my fabu and wildly expensive dress.

"What the fu…" I hissed as I slapped my own ass to put out the fire and slammed my backside up against a wall so my flaming butt wouldn't be noticed. Granted it was a small fire, but it didn't feel good. Clearly, the Goddess wasn't down with humans laying eggs even if they had called me a skank and had horrifying taste in witch-wear.

Shitballs.

I was training to be the next fucking Baba Yaga. Right now the fact that I had no intention of taking the job was irrelevant. At least the Goddess had only given me a tiny ass zap. Normally I was on the ground cursing like a sailor after one of her little *lessons*. She was actually being nice, if you could call shooting fire at someone's butt nice. I got the message loud and clear. Responsible witches didn't make humans lay eggs no matter how rude or poorly dressed they were.

Glancing back over my shoulder, I snapped my fingers and halted the poultry show. Thankfully, the room was teaming with magicians. If I got busted, I could play it off.

"What the heck?" a female voice shouted as I felt someone whack the back of my head.

First my ass and now my head? What the hell was happening? The temptation to turn around and zap whoever had the balls to whack me was high. However, my ass was still smoldering.

"Excuse me?" I snarled as I whipped around and my eyes landed on one of the most exquisite women I'd ever seen.

She was my height and had wavy jet-black hair that fell in

fabulous layers almost to her butt. Her eyes were redonk—the brightest and most crystal green I'd ever seen. She was dressed in a drop-dead green linen Prada dress that matched her otherworldly eyes.

The woman wore a wreath of sparkling green leaves in her hair—a seriously strange fashion choice, but she made it work. The hair ornament was so freakin' cool that I wondered if I should get one. It was far superior to all the fucking pointy hats at the convention.

And she was pissed. At me...

"Don't play games with me, Zach," she snapped. "I have no issues if you like to cross-dress, but it might have been something you wanted to share with me in private instead of at a public event."

"Lost here," I muttered, wondering what the heck she was and who the heck Zach was.

She wasn't human by a long shot. However, she wasn't a witch and definitely wasn't a Shifter. I'd never encountered anything like her. The angry woman packed a punch. I now had a headache *and* a singed ass. Not turning out to be my day so far.

"Oh, puhleeese," she said with an eye roll worthy of one of mine. "Playing hard to get is one thing. Pretending to be a woman is a little much. Don't you think, Zach?"

"I'm so fucking confused," I muttered, wondering if this one was causing the shenanigans.

"But I have to compliment you on the dress. Stella McCartney is the bomb and you look like a freakin' supermodel in it, but..."

And then she started to cry. I was still completely bewildered by the conversation but she pulled at my heartstrings. Why? No clue. Goddess, being happy was making me soft. The old me would have zapped her bald and moved on. The new me wanted to *help*. Shit.

"Umm… I'm not Zach," I said, snapping my fingers and handing her a wad of tissue.

"Yeah, right," she said, taking the tissue and blotting her eyes. "If you don't like me, just tell me. I'm fully aware that I've been chasing you for years and you haven't caved, but I was beginning to think you might like me a little bit."

Squinting my eyes at her and glancing around, I sighed. Whatever she was had now made herself one of my problems. The Zach dude was a fucking idiot. This gal was gorgeous, gave excellent eye roll, and had incredible taste in clothes. Under different circumstances, I would ask her to go shopping with me. However, I didn't think that would go over real well at the moment.

"Okay, if you promise not to hit me again, I promise not to turn your hair purple and give you a mullet," I told her, backing away just in case.

"Whatever," she said, blowing her nose and then handing me back the wad of tissue.

"I'm good. You can keep that." I almost took the snotty tissue back. Being a mom, snot wasn't as much of an issue as it used to be for me. But I really didn't want to handle a stranger's mucus no matter how well she was dressed.

"My bad," she replied with a small smile and a few tears still rolling down her cheeks. "You look great as a woman. Your boobs even look real. Can I touch them?"

"Duuuude," I said, slapping her hand away as she went for a grab. "The knockers are real. I'm not Zach."

She cocked her head to the side and stared at me in surprise. "Your boobs are real?"

"Yessss," I said with an eye roll. "You can't fake perfection like these knockers.

"They are really nice."

"Thank you."

"You're welcome," she said politely.

It was a standoff of sorts. We stood motionless amidst an array of counterfeit mummies, witches and vampires who were perusing the goods at the largest indoor magic shit shop I'd ever witnessed. They did not need to hear this conversation. It was obvious she still didn't believe I wasn't Zach.

"You're a woman?"

"Last time I checked, yes," I told her, grabbing her hand and pulling her to a less populated area. If she wasn't the shenanigans, I had a feeling she could help me find them. She was the most magical person I'd come across so far. Although, I still couldn't place what she was.

"So you're *really* not Zach?" she questioned, shaking her head in confusion as she stared at me.

"Not Zach," I confirmed. "And I'd like to add that he must be a douchewagon not to like you."

"Thank you," she said with the beginnings of another smile. "Who are you? I mean, I can tell you're a witch—a really powerful one at that—but..."

"I'm Zelda. Who are you?"

"Willow," she replied, touching my hair. "Is this your real color?"

"Oh, my Goddess, first my boobs and now my hair? Yessss, it's my real color. Why?"

"Zach's hair color is *exactly* the same... and his eyes and his face...the same too. I mean, not his body. He doesn't have boobs," she explained.

"Well, if the assmonkey's name is Zach, I would hope not," I shot back wondering if Willow was right in the head. "What are you?"

She eyed me for a long moment and then giggled. "I'm not allowed to tell."

"Says who?" I demanded. After being zapped and whacked, I was in no mood for cryptic bullshit.

"The Goddess," she said reverently. "Anyone who is to know my true origin has to discover it on their own."

The cryptic rules in the magical world drove me nuts. "Does Zach know?"

Her lovely chin dropped to her chest and she sighed. "No. He won't let me get close enough to him in a spiritual sense to learn my secret."

"Can I ask you a question?"

"Sure, Zelda."

"Why are you pining away for an idiot who doesn't see your worth?" I asked. Did she have terrible self-esteem? Was she one of those gals who only went for the unavailable guys? Was Zach a human?

"Interesting," she said with a small chuckle. "Do you realize what you just said?"

"Umm… yes?"

"Were you trying to guess my origin? Because that was close."

I went back over my last sentence in my head and decided Willow was crazy—possibly batshit crazy, but for some reason I liked her. "Nope, and you're avoiding the question."

"He's my mate," she said with a sad smile. "He needs me."

Okay, she was either some serious cray-cray, a stalker of this Zach dude, or she was telling the truth. Since I still had no clue what the fuck I was looking for, I decided this could be a good distraction, or it could lead me to why I was at the dumbass Witchypoo Convention in the first place.

"Is Zach here?" I asked.

"He is," she said nodding happily. "He's with Zorro… and his *mother*."

Her tone changed dramatically when she said the word *mother*. It wasn't reverent. Willow's voice was odd and somewhat resentful. Interesting.

"Is that supposed to mean something to me?" I inquired,

hoping Sassy was behaving herself and that my cats weren't fornicating in public.

"Everyone knows Zorro," she said with a giggle. "He's kind of famous around here."

"Well, I'm not from here," I told her. "I'm just in town for the umm… festivities." It was the most neutral way to describe the joke of a convention.

"You're the real deal. Why are you here?" Willow asked, touching my hair again.

"I could ask you the same question," I pointed out, feeling strangely fine that someone I had just met was playing with my hair.

She smiled and stood up straight. Willow was taller than I'd thought originally or she'd just grown a few inches. "I'm here because Zach is here. He comes to all of these silly magic shitshows."

Willow was clearly my kind of gal with the use of the word shitshow. Of course, the next question was why? Why did Zach come to gatherings like these?

My guess? *Shenanigans.*

Getting smacked by Willow was turning out to be a fine thing indeed.

"And what does Zach do at these shitshows?"

"He does nothing," Willow explained. "It's his mother. She reads palms—goes by Marie Laveau, if you can believe that crap."

A foreboding tingle skittered up my spine and I had to keep my hands from sparking with effort. Was Willow involved with the bloodletting? Was I being set up? My gut said no, but my gut had also told me to buy gauchos a few years back when some asshole reported in *Glamour* that they were coming back into style. My gut could be wrong sometimes—very wrong. I had six pairs of gauchos that proved that theory.

I could sense Willow had strong magic, but she had no clue

how powerful I was, and I wasn't about to inform her. I was loaded with more light and dark magic that should be legally allowed. Right now I was very happy about that.

Reaching into my pocket, I felt for my walkie talkie. I knew I could call for Sassy, Mac or Jeeves in a heartbeat. I also knew I didn't necessarily need them. I could blow Rupp Arena sky high with a wiggle of my nose. However, that was exactly why I needed them. Subtlety wasn't my finest quality.

"Since I'm new in town, why don't you introduce me to Zach and Zorro?" I suggested. "Oh, and Marie Laveau."

"Marie Laveau *aka* Henrietta Smith will be sequestered in her tent," Willow informed me with another impressive eye roll. "But I'd bet we could find Zorro."

"And Zach?" I asked with a raised brow.

Willow sighed and blushed. "Yes. Zorro is never far from Zach."

"Great. Let's go."

Let the shenanigans begin…

CHAPTER NINE

"Holy shee-ot, guuuurlfriend! Zach?" a ridiculously handsome Shifter shouted in delighted shock. "I had no clue you were into *that*. The boobies are to *die* for."

Zorro—I assumed—was dressed from head to toe in purple leather. It was just on the edge of wrong, but he made it work. If I had to guess, I'd say he liked boys, not girls. I had no problem whatsoever with that, but it was unusual to meet a gay Shifter. I wondered if he had a pack and I also wondered if Willow was blind... Maybe the elusive Zach was a gay Shifter too.

"Duuude," I snapped at the grinning Zorro. "I am not Zach. I'm Zelda. My girls are real and I'm a little tired of being mistaken for a man. It is not good for my fucking ego. You feel me?"

Zorro's laugh was all kinds of charming. I understood immediately why he was popular around town.

"Well, slap my fine leather covered ass and call me Sally," Zorro said, staring at me like I had two heads. "You're really not Zach in a fabu dress?"

I rolled my eyes. "Nope. Not Zach. And what are you?"

I was well aware that he was a Shifter, but I couldn't tell

exactly which kind. Mac would have known in a second, but Mac wasn't here.

"I'm gay," he replied waggling his eyebrows.

"Not what I meant," I replied, now smiling at the nutty man.

"Whoopsie, my bad. Let me be more specific. I'm not really a *club gay*. I'm more of a stay at home *couch gay*. I like to refer to myself as a homosectional."

His laugh at his own joke was loud. It made me feel warm and fuzzy. Holding back my own grin was impossible. I really hoped Willow and Zorro weren't the bad guys here. It would suck all kinds of ass to have to eliminate them.

"While that's great to know," I said, still grinning. "I was referring to your species."

"Ohhhhh, I see we're getting *personal* here. No worries gurlfriend. I'm a goat Shifter. A fainting goat Shifter. A gay fainting goat Shifter."

"Shut the front fucking door," I said, gaping at the beautiful, sandy blond haired, blue eyed man. Not one mummy, vampire or witch even blinked an eye at Zorro's confession. Since they were all lying about what they were, they clearly assumed everyone else was too. "For real?"

"For reals, for reals," Zorro said with a wink. "I'm the one that passes out in a crisis. You know, so everyone can get away and the predator will eat me."

"Oh, my Goddess," I choked out. "That must suck."

"Back in the day when I actually had to work, it did suck," Zorro said, admiring my shoes and abruptly changing the subject. "What size are those Jimmy Choos?"

"Seven and a half," I told him.

"Damnit, I'm a nine. I would rock those heels."

And that's when my pocket started talking.

"You know, if you were going to have a freakin' sex change at the Poop Convention, you might have wanted to give me a heads up." Sassy's shrill voice came in loud and clear through the fabric. "I mean, you look hot and all, but Mac might be a little put out."

"Dude," I snapped, grabbing the walkie-talkie out of my pocket and pressing the button. "I'm still a girl."

"No you're not," Sassy corrected me.

"Am."

"Not."

"I am."

"Zelda, I'm following you down an aisle filled with horny mummies," she informed me. "You are not answering to your name. And I just stepped in a pile of fucking eggs. What gives, dude?"

I rolled my eyes as Zorro and Willow listened to the exchange with fascination. I wanted to ask her how she knew the mummies were horny, but I was terrified of her answer. I kind of liked my new buddies and I didn't want them to get completely *Sassied* quite yet. "Is the person you're following talking on a walkie-talkie?" I asked, hoping logic wouldn't make her blow something up.

"Holy shit. NO. How are you doing that? Are you a ventricle?" she demanded.

I sighed. "I'm not a fluid filled brain cavity."

"Are you speaking Canadian? You know I'm not fluent in fucking Canadian."

"My bad," I said with an eye roll. "Where is the person that you're following going?"

"Well, since it's you, I would think you could answer that question. But from what I can tell you're headed to the far back left corner." Sassy griped. "And you're walking fucking fast. SLOW DOWN. I'm wearing Prada stilettos, for the love of the Goddess."

"Just keep following me," I instructed her. I was already in the far back left corner. Apparently, Zach was headed this way.

"Zach is coming," Willow whispered to Zorro. "Is she here?"

Zorro shook his head and was no longer the happy go lucky gay goat. "She's gone for an hour or so. Said she had some errands to run," he said tightly.

"And she let Zach stay here? Alone?" Willow asked, shocked.

Goddess, Zach sounded like a momma's boy… possibly a gay momma's boy. However, there must be something redeeming about the loser. Both Zorro and Willow seemed to adore the…

I realized I still had no clue what Zach was.

"Is Zach a Shifter?" I asked, scanning the crowd for a dude who resembled me followed by a pissed off Sassy with raw egg on her shoes.

"No," Willow said. "He's a warlock."

"And his mother is a witch?" I pressed, wanting more info. I was fairly sure Willow and Zorro weren't causing the shenanigans. Which led me to believe that Zach and his bloodletting mother were the problem.

"Human," Zorro said so quietly I was sure I'd heard him wrong.

"Human?" I asked, wrinkling my nose.

Zorro nodded.

"That's not possible," I replied. Something was very fishy here.

A warlock born to a human? Zorro must have his facts wrong. I knew witches could breed with any species of magical being, but a human? That was something I'd never heard of.

Then when my world tilted on its axis. Time slowed and I forgot where I was for a moment. My body tingled and some inside me felt strangely whole. WTF?

Zach approached, and I came face to face… with myself.

"What the hell?" Zach demanded dumbstruck, staring at me in absolute shock—the same way I stared right back at him.

It was even more like looking in a mirror than when I was with Fabio. Gazing at the warlock in front of me stole my ability to take a breath. My skin heated and my stomach churned. Were there fun house mirrors here?

"Who are you?" I whispered as I longed to reach out and touch him. I didn't dare. This could be a deadly trick.

"I should ask you the same question," he replied warily, stuffing his hands in his pockets.

Did he have the same desire to touch me?

We circled each other slowly until Zorro grabbed Zach and Willow grabbed me. They quickly led us into a large, ornately decorated tent. Sassy burst through the flaps right as Willow went to zip them shut.

"Zelda," she started and then froze. "What the hey hey? Is that Fabio?"

"Who's Fabio?" Zorro asked.

"A warlock," I said absently still completely absorbed in Zach and not wanting all my cards on the table… yet. "You're a healer?"

Zach nodded curtly and offered me a seat. All redheaded witches and warlocks were healers. The witches were more powerful than the warlocks, but both had the gift to repair and cure other magicals. I knew it was rude, but there was no way I could sit down. A part of me wanted to crawl out of my skin. I didn't know why, but something was very wrong.

"Age?" Zach demanded.

"That's kinda impolite," Sassy muttered.

I agreed, but I wanted to know the same thing. "Thirty-one," I replied and watched him pale.

"And you?" I shot back.

"The same."

I had to pace. If I didn't I was going to have a meltdown.

My mind raced with possible reasons for this. Did my dad have a bunch of random kids he didn't know about? That was feasible as he didn't know about me, but I was shocked that Fabio would have had sex with a human woman. It also would have meant he was boinking Zach's mother at the same time he was boinking mine since we were both thirty-one. Fabio had been randy in his past, but I didn't think he was that much of a man whore.

Could Zach and I be related? Could my dead Aunt Hildy have had a son and given him up for adoption? That was fucking ludicrous. Aunt Hildy never would have given her child away. She had been the most loving woman I'd ever known.

Zach *had* to be the product of my dad's overactive pecker. Possibly... or maybe not. I didn't know any other healing witches other than the ones I was related to. Maybe we all looked alike. My dad and I certainly did.

Instead of getting mad at Fabio for his possibly shady history of playing hide-the-salami, which may have resulted in Zach, I glanced around the large tent. The interior was creepy. Animal skulls and vials of blood lined the red and black shelves. Sawdust covered the floor and a few black braided rugs were scattered around. Candles flickered on every surface and a bogus crystal ball sat atop a blood red table in the center of the area. This was clearly where the bloodletting was going on.

"Are you responsible for this?" I demanded, pointing at the vials of blood and pushing down my need to know more about the warlock who was the mirror image of me.

"I don't see how that's any of your business," Zach said flatly. "Your name is Zelda?"

I nodded, not liking his attitude or tone of voice much, but still wanting desperately to touch his face. "Your birthday?"

"June twenty-second," he said, watching me closely.

That's when I sat down. It was either sit or drop to the ground with an ungraceful thud.

"Holy shit," Sassy shouted. "That's *your* birthday, Zelda. What are the fucking chances of that?"

"Slim to none," Zach muttered.

"Your father?" I asked, holding my breath.

His beautiful face went from neutral to a sneer of disgust. "No clue and don't give a shit. You?"

My stomach plummeted. He was me a few years ago. No wonder Zach wouldn't give Willow a chance. He didn't love himself. He couldn't love anyone else. I was a pro on that shit.

"A warlock named Fabio," I told him. "Your mother is the palm reader?"

"She is," he said emotionlessly. "And it's time for you to leave since she will be arriving back soon."

Zach stood and unzipped the tent flaps. Zorro and Willow appeared surprised at his rude behavior but seemed eager for us to leave as well. Without saying a word, he ushered Sassy out. I had no plans to leave, but Zach had other thoughts.

"You have to go," he insisted in a clipped tone. "Now. Do not come back here. Ever."

"Zach," Zorro said, narrowing his eyes at him. "You could be *related* to Zelda. What are you doing?"

"I think she's your twin," Willow said the words I'd been thinking.

But that was impossible. I was the only child of Fabio and Judith... or Sandy... or Isobelle... or Cassandra. My egg donor had gone by many names over her hundreds of years.

Zach looked at the ceiling for a brief moment and I thought he was going to cave. He didn't. When his eyes met mine, they were furious. Part of me wanted to cry and part of me wanted to throat punch him. My emotions were a rollercoaster at the moment.

Zach's magic began to show. Bright golden sparks filled the

tent and he growled low in his throat causing both Zorro and Willow to step back in fear. However, I wasn't scared of him. His anger was wildly evident, but I didn't think it was aimed at me. I could also smite his ill-mannered ass to hell and back with a wiggle of my finger.

His frustration verged on a magical meltdown. This dude could definitely use a few sessions with my therapist, Roger the rabbit. What I didn't need was Zach blowing all of our covers. What I did need was more information and I knew how to get it.

"Fine," I snapped, glaring at the ruder male version of myself. "I'll leave right now so you can be with your mommy. However, we're not done here, *Zach*. I'll be taking Zorro and Willow with me."

"Are you going to hurt them?" he growled. Bright blue sparkling fire engulfed his fingertips and his eyes glowed dangerously.

"There's a far better chance they'll be harmed by you right now," I shot back as my own magic began to swirl around me, mixing with his and making it hard to breathe in the confined space.

"Go with her," Zach ground out to Zorro and Willow. "She's right. You'll be safer."

Zorro shook his head and ran his hands through his hair. "If I'm not here, it will be bad for you."

"I'm fine," Zach snapped. "Go. Now. I will find you tonight."

There was so much more to this story than met the naked eye. And I was going to get to the bottom of it.

With a wave of his hand, Zach blew us out of the tent. It took me by surprise and I wasn't able to counter it. Zorro, Willow and I landed in a heap and knocked Sassy and her new blue broom to the floor.

"Fuck me running in platform boots," Zorro hissed as he

shoved all of us under a table covered in wands across from the tent. Getting under the table with us, he pressed his finger to his lips. "Not a word. No matter what happens… not a word."

I could have sworn Willow's fabu leafy hair ornament began to grow little vines with thorns, but I wasn't sure as it was kind of dark and crowded under the table. Shit was getting real. I wasn't sure what the shit was, but it felt very real.

"Out of my way," a harsh female voice demanded. "Marie Laveau is here."

Peeking out from under the table, I saw her. Again, breathing was difficult. Sassy grabbed my arm and silently dug her nails into me. There was a strange and bizarre evil in the air. The woman's magic was wrong. I was pretty sure Sassy broke the skin on my arm, but my brain was such a jumbled mess I didn't care. Marie Laveau *aka* Henrietta Smith was a showstopper—a wicked showstopper. Beautiful didn't begin to describe her. Her colorful robes flowed behind her as she moved with such grace it was if she was dancing.

However, there was no way in hell she was Zach's *mother*.

Nope. Her skin was a stunning mocha color and her hair was as black as night. And while the woman wasn't exactly a kind of witch I recognized, she most definitely knew about the secret world that existed around her.

I was certain the shenanigans had arrived.

CHAPTER TEN

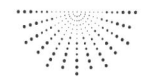

"We need to have a little chat," I said to Willow and Zorro, as I paced the living room of our hotel suite.

The tension in the air was thick. But I was fairly positive it was individual and internal. We were all having our own personal panic attack—except Sassy. Sassy was polishing her new freakin' broom with loving care.

"I agree," Zorro said cautiously. His body language was easy, but his unusual eyes were very serious.

Zorro's vertical pupils were slightly off-putting, but I'd gotten used to them quickly. The straight up and down black line in the center of the vivid blue was really kind of exotic and cool. Zorro was a goat after all. However, that didn't mean I trusted him or Willow—nor did they trust me.

None of us were really sure what each other's intentions were. I could pull the *Baba Yaga in training* card, but that was a *very* last resort.

Mac and Jeeves hadn't reported back yet, but there was still another hour and a half before we were supposed to meet up. My cats? The fat fuckers were nowhere to be found. My guess was that they had found some feline hookers. I really hoped they slapped a coat on it because I wasn't about to raise their illegitimate kittens.

"What is it you want to know?" Willow asked as she glanced over at Zorro with concern.

Willow, Zorro and Sassy sat in a row on the couch. Sassy had immediately tried out her new blue broom when we'd gotten to the suite. Thankfully, the ceilings were high. She'd only busted two lamps.

"Goddess, you smell good," Sassy said, sniffing Zorro. "Very minty."

Zorro grinned and patted Sassy on the head. "Thank you, gal pal. It's new. Never understood the appeal of peppermint body wash until this morning. Feels like my butthole smoked a menthol cigarette."

"TMI, goat," I said with a laugh.

"Whoopsie," Zorro said, easing the tension in the room. "I do tend to go on a bit."

Sassy sniffed him again and sighed happily. "I thought that was very descriptive. Your French is wonderful. Zelda can be a hardass, but since she's training to be the next…."

"Shifter Wanker with the most-est," I said cutting Sassy off and hoping she'd get it.

"Wait," Sassy said narrowing her eyes. "I thought…"

"Thinking. Is. Overrated," I said, giving her the eyeball.

"Are you speaking Canadian?"

Blowing out a long sigh, I simply nodded. "I'm the Shifter Wanker—*only* the Shifter Wanker. I heal idiots. However, right now I'm feeling the need to inflict some pain on an idiot."

I closed my eyes and clasped my hands together so I didn't snap my fingers and shove Sassy's new broom up her ass and yank it out of her overactive mouth. If she kept talking, she'd reveal our bra sizes.

"Who's the idiot?" Sassy asked with wide eyes. "I've got your back. I will kick the idiot's ass. Just point me at the bastard."

"Go look in the mirror in the bathroom," I told her. If she left the room, I wouldn't give her a pair of testicles attached to her forehead. Also, it would take her at least an hour of looking for someone hiding in the mirror before she either realized it was her or she decided the idiot was too camouflaged to find.

Grabbing her broom, Sassy sprinted to the bathroom. Willow bit down on her bottom lip trying not to laugh. Zorro just smiled.

"She's not that clever, but she's loyal and she can cast spells like a motherhumper, among other witchy things," I said and then held my hand up before they could comment in any kind of insulting way. "And I love her. The idiot is my BBF—mostly by default because we spent nine months in the pokey together for misuse of magic. But that being said, I can talk smack on her all I want because she's mine. I like you guys, but if you say anything bad about the imbecile, I will zap your asses so hard you won't sit for six months. Cool?"

Zorro laughed and made himself comfortable on the couch. "I hear you loud and clear, gurlfriend. I like you too. You're my kind of fabulously dressed, semi-violent asskicker."

"Well… thank you," I replied. "I've only been nice for a little over a year. I'm still seriously materialistic—which I'm kind of working on. But my uncaring reputation has suffered since my therapy sessions and being insanely happy. Orgasms help too."

Willow was giggling and Zorro didn't have the haunted look in his eyes that I'd seen at Rupp Arena. However, there were many secrets being kept here.

"Zach's mother is not a human," I stated, getting the ball rolling.

"She is," Zorro disagreed. "And I worry for your safety."

Shaking my head, I realized they didn't understand. They weren't witches. And my safety was the last of my concerns right now. Little did my new friends know I was very good at taking care of myself *and* others. Right now my concern was Zach—his heritage and his guilt or innocence. "Okay, let's say for argument's sake she is human—which she's not—she couldn't have given birth to a warlock."

"She didn't give birth to Zach," Willow said slowly, looking to Zorro either for strength or approval.

"But she's his mother?" I pressed, not understanding.

"Why are you here, Zelda?" Willow inquired warily.

I stared at her for a moment and then decided to go with the truth—or most of it. If I wanted the truth from them, it was only fair that they got the same from me.

"I was sent here by Baba Yaga," I said slowly, waiting for their reactions.

They didn't disappoint.

"You know *the Baba Yaga?*" Zorro asked, awed as Willow worried at her bottom lip with her teeth. "Is she fabu?"

I rolled my eyes. "If you believe someone who is permanently stuck in the eighties—think Madonna wannabe—is fabu, then yes. And same rule applies to Baba Yojackhole. I can bash her big-haired ass till the cows come home. You guys? Not so much."

"Why did the leader of the witches send you?" Willow asked.

I paused and considered her question. "She wasn't sure why. Baba Yaga said there were shenanigans going on here."

"You got that right," Zorro said under his breath.

"We're *fine* here," Willow insisted as her leafy crown began to glow and spit little green sparks. She gave Zorro a harsh glance and he quickly glanced down at the floor.

"Bloodletting is *not fine*," I said flatly wondering why Willow was so unnerved and growing seriously uncomfortable.

"It's why Zach is still alive," Willow hissed as a pine scented wind began to swirl through the suite. "If you'd like to be the cause of his death, then by all means keep prying."

Zorro was not pleased. "Willow. Enough."

My hair began to blow around my head and my fingers began to spark ominously. My choices were slightly limited here. We were in a freakin' hotel loaded with humans. I could take Willow and Zorro prisoner, but the thought of that almost made me laugh. And I had no clue what Willow was other than really pretty with bizarre headwear. I wondered if Zorro knew…

"Guys, I'm about to do something here," I said, trying to pull back on my magic. "I'm gonna go with my gut. Not always the best idea since last week my gut told me to buy some chunky dad sneakers and some drop crotch pants because of a stupid ass article in *Elle Magazine*."

"You didn't," Zorro said with his hand over his mouth in horror.

"I did," I confirmed. "And they were on fucking sale, so I can't send them back. Soooo, as you can see, my gut can lead me astray. I would really suggest you start talking or Goddess only knows what could go down."

Zorro and Willow exchanged glances. Willow looked like she wanted to cry and Zorro appeared defeated. My stomach clenched and I felt just horrible.

"Henrietta is human," Zorro said. "She's well over a hundred and fifty."

"Not buying that," I said flatly. "She looks about thirty to me."

"It's true and it's why you have to leave."

"Not finding anyone in the mirror," Sassy called out from the bathroom.

"Keep looking," I yelled back. I turned back to Zorro and

Willow and narrowed my gaze. "And you need to keep talking if you don't want me to go all witchy on your asses."

"She takes Zach's blood to stay young. And the blood from humans mixed with Shifter blood gives her power," Willow blurted out as Zorro closed his eyes and nodded.

"Drinking the blood gives her a modicum of power which is why you don't sense a she's a human," Zorro confirmed. "If she sees another healer, she'll go after your blood as well. You need to leave town."

I was floored. And I was pissed. This made no sense. "Why would Zach give her his blood? And what the fuck kind of power does she have?"

Zorro shrugged. "Her power is unknown. But most of the Shifter community has left the area. The threat of exposure or death has scared them away. It's not safe here for any magical."

"Then why are you still here?" I asked, still unable to believe a human could wield any kind of power even if she was ingesting the blood of magicals and humans.

"Zach saved my life twenty years ago. A gay goat Shifter is of no value to his herd. I'll never reproduce. I was beaten and left for dead by my own kind," Zorro said with a small sad smile on his face. "I won't leave him to be drained dry by that woman. I'm the sacrificial lamb… or goat to be more specific."

"Explain," I ground out through clenched teeth as I turned away and blasted a hole through the wall. My fury almost overcame me. "Sorry. Had to let a little out so I don't take the building down."

"No worries," Zorro said with an understanding smile. "It's not a pretty tale."

"More," I said. I needed to hear this even if I didn't want to.

"Zach healed me when I was dying and I in turn heal him."

That was interesting… "You're a healer?"

Zorro chuckled and shook his head. "No. Not even close.

When she takes too much blood from Zach, my instincts kick in."

"Your instincts?" I wasn't following. It was such a bizarre plot line I didn't know what to make of it. However, I knew it sucked ass.

"I faint in times of distress," Zorro went on. "When she's about to drain Zach dry, I pass out and she goes for my blood. When she's done and Zach has recovered enough, he heals me."

I was right. This sucked all kinds of illegal and immoral ass.

"Duuuuude, I can end this shit right now," I said, blowing another hole in the wall. I chose a different wall. We were gonna have to pay a fucking fortune for the damage I was causing. However, replacing the entire hotel was out of the question. A few holes were keeping a lot of people safe. "I'll march right back over to Rump Arena and send that evil bee-otch to the Next Adventure... or more likely Hell."

"It's Rupp Arena," Zorro corrected me politely.

"Right. My bad. Rupp Arena. Just give me twenty minutes and this story will have a very happy ending," I promised.

"You can't," Willow gasped out and paled to the point I thought she was going to pass out. "He'll die."

"*Not Zach*," I told her. "Marie Henriette Laveau Smith. I can smite her ass like you've never seen. A quickie little spell with a healthy dose of profanity thrown in will solve it. No. Problem."

Zorro shook his head and ran his hands through his hair in agitation. "Willow is correct. If you eliminate Henrietta, you will also eliminate Zach."

The news was unwelcome and my reaction to it shocked me. My stomach cramped and I felt like a part of me was dying. WTF? "Pardon me for a sec," I growled.

Wiggling my nose, all of the furniture in the room began to fly and landed in a large heap in the middle of the suite. I left the couch that Willow and Zorro were sitting on alone. I did have a few manners. There was now a chair, TV, lamp, desk and end table pile. With a slash of my arm through the air, I incinerated the assemblage. The fire danced as flames engulfed the furniture. It relieved some of my stress, but I was still a ticking time bomb. Gold and silver glitter swirled around the room and a strong wind blew through knocking Willow and Zorro to the ground.

"I smell fire. Are you making s'mores without me?" Sassy yelled from the bathroom.

"No," I shouted and rolled my eyes. Snapping my fingers, I doused the flames. I didn't need a human fire department showing up. This would be kind of hard to explain.

"That was impressive," Zorro commented, getting to his feet and extending his hand to Willow.

I shrugged. "That was nothing," I shot back grimly. "Explain to me why Zach's life is connected to that woman's."

"Henrietta bought him," Zorro said woodenly. "She owns him."

"People don't own people," I snapped, wondering what pile of crap Zorro was trying to feed me.

"Zelda, you're thirty-one years old," Willow pointed out. "We're not. Many things that are wrong happen all the time."

"How old are you?" I demanded, trying to put pieces of an enormous puzzle together that made no sense at all.

"I'm a hundred and Zorro is seventy-five," Willow said.

"I know why Zorro stayed. Why did you?" I asked her.

"Because I love him," she whispered.

Her statement tore at my heart. However, since magicals stopped aging around thirty, their ages didn't shock me. But the *shockers* had just begun.

"Still not following why his life is connected," I snapped, needing to let a little more steam off so we would all survive the next few minutes. "Guys, could you move away from the couch please?"

"Certainly," Zorro replied quickly and pulled Willow a safe distance away.

Aiming my middle finger at the couch, it disintegrated to ash. Zorro and Willow watched with wide, shocked eyes.

"I'm good now," I said, expelling a long breath. "This shit is affecting me in weird ways."

"Wait," Willow said, getting excited as the leaves in her hair perked up and a few pink flowers appeared. "Can you break a spell?"

"What kind of spell?" I asked doubtfully, still wondering what the heck she was. "It would be safest if I knew who cast the spell."

"Not sure about any of that," she said, getting more excited. "Zach's life is connected to Henrietta's by some kind of enchantment."

"Cast by a human?" I asked.

"No," Zorro said. "It was cast when he was sold—by his birth mother."

The room began to spin and I sat down on the floor before my knees gave out and I fell. "Do you know who his *real* mother is?"

"We don't," Willow said, approaching me and touching my hair that was the identical shade of Zach's. "But I'm hoping maybe you do."

If Zach's birth mother was who I was beginning to this she was, this wasn't just a horrifying story. It was a fucking nightmare—even worse than the fact that she'd tried to kill me. If Zach was indeed the other half of me, she had killed both of us.

Was one woman truly capable of such vicious evil? Zach may have been kind of a jackhole to me earlier, but his life had been one of massive abuse. First at the hands of the *mother* who sold him, and then at the hands of the *mother* who used him.

There was only one way to find out if I was correct.

"Does Zach know who his egg donor was?" I whispered, still feeling ill.

"No," Zorro said. "Do you?"

"I think I might."

CHAPTER ELEVEN

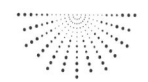

"Even if she cast the spell, she can't break it. Your mother is human now," Mac said, taking in the damage to our suite without commenting on it.

He eyed our guests and nodded politely. Surprisingly Zorro bowed low to Mac. Mac approached Zorro and titled his head as he noticed his eyes.

"Your name?" Mac asked.

"Zorro, your majesty," he said, bowing again. "And I must say you are *waaay finer* than the rumors make you out to be."

"Dude," I said with a laugh. "He's taken."

"Very taken." Mac grinned and winked at me. "And thank you," he said to Zorro.

Wait. Weird. How did Zorro know that Mac was the King of the Shifters in podunk Assjacket, West Virginia? Maybe he could scent it like an animal… Well, he was an animal. I then wondered if Mac noticed how minty fresh Zorro smelled. I really hoped Mac didn't ask about it. Not real sure he would think a menthol butthole was as funny as I did.

"You're the lone fainting goat I was told about?" Mac asked, still watching Zorro with interest.

"I am."

Mac nodded and glanced over at Willow. "And you?"

"Willow," she replied.

"Does Zelda realize what you are?" Mac inquired, glancing over at me with interest.

"Oh, my Goddess," I griped. "You can tell what Willow is and I can't?"

"Apparently," Mac said with a chuckle as he pulled me close and laid a quick hot one on my mouth.

My lips tingled and my girlie parts perked up, but then I remembered the shitshow unfolding and groaned. Hotel sex was going to have to wait. Shit.

"Can you give me a hint about Willow?"

Mac squinted and gave me one of his smiles that made me forget my name. "Nope, baby. Not allowed."

I thought about offering up a blowjob in exchange for the information, but there were far too many people in the room. And I didn't think it would work anyway. Not that I wasn't fabulous at giving Mac blowjobs. I was. But if the Goddess caught wind that I was trading sexual favors for intel she might zap my mouth shut. Which would suck—bad pun intended.

"Fine," I said, pouting—more about the fact that I wasn't going to get to play *The Princess and the Penis* in a hotel than I was about not learning Willow's secret. If Mac wasn't alarmed by Willow's species then I wasn't going to be either. I'd figure it out eventually. "So Willow will remain a mystery for the time being. How in the heck does Zorro know who you are?"

"My father is not only the King of the Shifters in Assjacket…" Jeeves said with a proud smile.

"Shut the front door. *What?*" I asked, gaping at Mac. "How did I not know this? So you're like the freakin' Baba Yaga of Shifters?"

"I am," Mac said with a grin.

"Dude, that is so hot," I said, really wishing we were alone. And then I froze. "Our kids are so fucked."

"How so?" Zorro inquired.

Without thinking, I let it rip. So much for holding onto any secrets. "Because I'm supposed to take over for Baba Yobutthole eventually and rule the most insane species known to the Universe and Mac is in charge of a shitload of clumsy, hairy freaks. Our babies will be saddled with some heavy shit eventually. Not to mention, this is really gonna cut in on nookie time."

I froze again, but this time in embarrassment. "Sorry," I told Zorro and Jeeves. "Didn't mean to insult you guys."

"No offense taken, Zelda," Jeeves said, bouncing on his toes and chuckling. "Mostly because your assessment is correct."

"Okaaaaay," Sassy grumbled, finally coming out of the bathroom looking frazzled. "I can't find anyone in the mirror that deserves an ass kicking. However, I'd like to come clean before I get busted. I tried on all your lingerie and pilfered your NARS Orgasm After Glow lip gloss. I totally rock it."

"There are people in the mirror?" Mac asked, perplexed.

It wasn't an odd question considering what we all were, but explaining would take too long and possibly piss Sassy off. Since there was very little left to break or blow up in the suite, I decided not to expound on my *keeping Sassy busy* tactics.

"Apparently not," I told him, giving him the side eye so he didn't press for more.

Thankfully, he got it.

"Are you sure that this Zach person is related to you?" Mac asked, getting back on track.

I was about to say no, but the word literally wouldn't come out of my mouth. I tried again. Again, I was mute. Mac observed me as I tried yet one more time to say no. I looked like an idiot. WTF?

"If you're trying to be a ventricle, it's not working," Sassy pointed out.

"Zip it, jackhole," I snapped and tried to say no again. I failed.

"Zach and Zelda are practically identical," Willow offered as she too noticed my bizarre dilemma. "The resemblance is almost mirror perfect—and then of course they have matching birthdays and ages."

Mac's head jerked to me in surprise. "Same age and birthday?"

"Yes," I confirmed wondering why I could say yes and not no. "Ask me if I like tofu."

"You hate tofu," Mac reminded me.

"I know that." I rolled my eyes. "Just ask me please."

"Okay. Do you like tofu?"

"NO," I shouted making everyone in the room jump including myself. "Now ask me if I'm related to Zach."

"Are you related to Zach?" he asked, eyeing me with concern.

I wanted to say no, but it wouldn't pass my lips. "Ask something more specific about Zach."

Willow got it. She smiled and I could have sworn she grew another inch. Not to mention tiny purple flowers had sprouted in her hair along with the pink. "Is Zach your twin brother?"

I closed my eyes and envisioned myself saying no. I could see it. If I could think it, I could say it. Right?

Wrong.

It had to be the Goddess at work here. However, I needed to test that theory too.

"Everybody back up," I instructed, gritting my teeth and steeling myself for some pain.

Without asking a single question, all the occupants of the room quickly backed themselves against the walls—all except Sassy.

"Umm… dude?" I said, squinting at her.

"Yes, dude?" Sassy asked, still holding her new blue broom.

"I was definitely speaking English when I told everyone to move."

"Yep," she agreed and didn't budge an inch.

"So move."

"No can do, buttwad. I can tell you're about to do something that's gonna hurt like a motherfucker. I'm here to absorb some of your stupid. That's what BFFs are for."

Sassy could render me mute for many reasons. This was one of them. I loved the idiot.

"You sure?" I asked, looking at her askance.

"Yep. Plus I also swiped your Urban Decay Naked eye shadow palette. It's only fair."

Well, when she put it that way…

Raising my arms to the sky, I felt my light magic flow through me. My skin began to shimmer and golden sparkles bounced around the room. A breeze tossed the magic around and I felt freer than I had all day.

Goddess on high, just checking in.
I might have a brother—maybe a twin.
If Zach is indeed mine,
Please give me a sign… and preferably not on my fucking
    behind.
In you, I shall trust,
What I plan will not bust.
In your wisdom and love, please send me a token.
And though I heard you wear mom jeans… I will know you
    have spoken.

"So mote it be," Sassy said, giving me a high five. "Zel, the way you get the word fucking into all of your spells is truly inspired. The mom jeans thing was also excellent."

"It didn't really fit, but I kinda just went with the flow," I told her.

"You rocked it, dude,"

"Thank you," I said right before the bolt of bright magenta lightning connected with my ass.

"Holy shitballs," Sassy shouted as she whacked my flaming butt with her new broom.

Sassy had one hell of an arm. I wasn't sure at this point what hurt more, the ass zap or the attempt to put it out. Unfortunately, Sassy was on a fucking mission and the whacks kept coming.

"Enough," I shouted as I turned Sassy's bushy stick of torture into a pillow with a wave of my hand. "I don't need a burnt *and* concave butt, you assmonkey."

"My bad," Sassy apologized as she snapped her fingers and created a small monsoon over my lower half.

My Stella McCartney was now as soaked as was I, but the flames were out. The dress was a goner anyway. I could feel the large hole in the back. This sucked. I really liked the dress. For a second, I thought about repairing it with magic, but I didn't dare. Part of my parole requirement was to use magic for others and not on material things for myself. Even with my ass hanging out for all to see, I wasn't about to test if the terms of my parole still stood. Besides, I kind of liked the rule—not that I would ever admit it.

"Blanket," I requested as I crawled to my feet and put my hands over my exposed derriere. "Or another Stella McCartney if anyone has one laying around."

Willow clapped her hands and in the blink of an eye, I was dry and dressed in the most rockin' Alice and Olivia mini dress I'd ever seen.

"I know you like Stella, but I was positive you would kill this little number," Willow said with a grin.

"Oh. My. Goddess," I shrieked as I sprinted over to the full-length mirror on the back of the door and checked myself out from every angle. "I am so hot!"

"That you are, little witch," Mac said with a chuckle as he pulled me away from the mirror. "I think you got your sign from the Goddess."

"And a new scar on my ass to go with it," I muttered as I took one more peek at my new fabu dress. "Willow, you are now in the club, my friend."

Sassy admired my dress with envy. "Umm… if I set myself on fire, can I have a new dress too?"

Willow giggled. "Sassy, that pink Prada is smoking hot without a fire. How about you keep that dress and I'll whip you up a new one for tomorrow?"

"Deal!" Sassy squealed and then glanced over forlornly at the body-sized pillow that used to be her blue broom.

"Shit," I mumbled as I stared at her. She was willing to absorb some of my stupid. I had to be willing to fix hers. "Here's the deal, dude. I'll change it back if you swear on Witch's Honor that shit stick will never come near my ass again in this lifetime."

"Promise," Sassy said with a giggle.

"I can fix it," Willow volunteered. "I'm very good with wood."

Another hint?

"Willow," Zorro said, catching her hand in his before she cast a spell. "You're depleting yourself and we're not near a forest."

Hmm… interesting.

"No worries. I've got it," I said, wiggling my nose and turning the pillow back into the broom. I didn't comment on the clues because I still had no idea what the heck Willow was. However, I filed them away. She'd blow her cover sooner or later. "I need to talk to Zach."

"Henrietta will fall into a deep sleep this evening after all the blood she's taken today," Zorro said with a shudder. "Zach will come and find Willow and me after she's out."

"Where?" I asked, totally repulsed at the story.

"In the forest," Willow replied, watching me carefully.

"Of course," I said with an eye roll. "'Cause nothing *bad* ever happens in the forest after dark when witches are involved."

Zorro simply smiled and shrugged. "It's the only place that will protect us."

"Meaning?" I asked.

Zorro and Willow exchanged smiles. "Come and you will see," he said, handing me a card.

It had an address on the front and a map on the back. There was a small X in the middle of the map.

"X marks the spot," Willow said. "We will meet you there this evening at the witching hour."

"We'll be there," Mac said to our guests as my mind raced with everything that could possibly go wrong—including that Zorro and Willow might be lying and this could be a dead end. My gut said they were for real, but it had already been established how wrong my gut could be.

"Excellent," Zorro said as he leaned in to give me a hug.

The pain I felt when his body made contact with mine was hundreds of times worse than the message from the Goddess. I gasped as my insides felt like they were being shredded with a hot knife.

"Fuck," I choked out as I doubled over in agony.

Mac, misunderstanding, tackled Zorro to the ground and held him in a death grip. Willow screamed and tried to pull Mac off. Moving Mac was literally impossible.

"Stop," I hissed at Mac. "Zorro didn't try to harm me. Please Mac, release him."

"Then what did I just see?" Mac ground out through

clenched teeth as Zorro's face began to turn as purple as his leather ensemble.

"You saw the Shifter Wanker in action," I said, crawling over to Zorro and gently removing Mac's hands from his neck. "I felt his pain. He didn't try to hurt me." I turned my attention to a frightened and gasping Zorro. "What has been done to you?"

He tried to smile, but it didn't reach his unusual eyes. My own eyes filled with tears and my entire body burned with pain. Zorro was so damaged internally it was horrifying. How was he even alive?

"It's nothing, gurlfriend," Zorro insisted in a hoarse voice. "I'm fine."

"You are not fucking fine," I hissed as I began to run my hands over his chest and stomach and then back to his head. Shit. If this was left over from his near-death beating twenty years ago, Zach wasn't much of a healer. However, I didn't think so. It was too raw to be old wounds. "What does that woman do to you when you're passed out?" I demanded as my fingers began to spark with fury.

Zorro closed his eyes and took a few deep breaths. "I don't know, doll," he admitted hollowly. "I'm not exactly awake, but it takes days to recover when I come to."

Willow stood silently beside Zorro's prone body and cried. The leaves in her hair wilted and the flowers had turned brown. It was killing me not to know what she was, but I had more important matters to deal with first.

Cracking my neck and my knuckles, I looked to Mac. He nodded curtly and stepped back.

"My apologies, Zorro," Mac said gruffly.

"None necessary, your majesty," Zorro replied with a respectful nod. "Zelda is your world and you thought I'd harmed her. I get it. I would do the same for Zach and Willow."

"Apparently, you already do. Mac, can you and Willow remove his clothes? Leave his underwear on. It would be easier if Zorro shifted, but I'm worried that he won't be able to come out of it. I'm gonna fix him in his human form," I said as I closed my eyes and began to chant softly. I'd never healed someone with this many injuries at the same time before. It was going to suck some major ass, but that was just too bad. "Hang on Zorro. This will hurt like a mofo and then it won't. Don't fight me, okay?"

"Wait. Will this deplete you?" Zorro asked in a worried tone as he tried to stop Mac and Willow from removing his clothes. "If so, please save your strength for Zach. I'm fine. This is my normal."

"Not any fucking more it's not," I said, gently touching his cheek. "Close your eyes and give into me."

"Thank you, gurlfriend" he whispered with a sad smile. "You're a beautiful witch—inside and out."

As I laid my hands on him, I thought I might faint or throw up. I didn't. Instead, I took in the most excruciating pain I'd ever experienced as a healer. His kidneys were severely bruised and damaged. Zorro's heart had holes in it as if it had been pricked with hundreds of tiny needles.

I gulped air as I tried to get through the pain of mending his cracked skull and spine back together. How in the Goddesses name had the goat even been able to stand, much less make a coherent sentence? His arms looked like he was a drug addict. Needle holes dotted the entire landscape of his arms and legs. I wanted to kill Henrietta Marie Laveau Smith so fucking dead and somehow I was going to do just that. But first I had to fix the goat.

"A little more," I gasped out to a deathly pale Zorro. "Just a few more minutes."

He nodded his head and screwed his eyes shut even tighter. If it felt this bad for me, I couldn't imagine how it felt for him.

Mending his stomach and lower intestines, I felt dizzy with

exhaustion. The last part was healing the deep purple bruises that covered his body. Slowly and gently, I ran my hand over each vicious mark.

"Gonna get sick," I said, grabbing for Mac.

Without a word, the man I loved more than any other in the world quickly scooped me up in his arms and sprinted to the bathroom. He held my hair back as I emptied the contents of my stomach into the toilet. Healing a Shifter had never made me sick before, but this hadn't been an ordinary healing. Mac gently rubbed my back as I cried about all of the horrible things that had happened to Zorro. I wasn't even sure what had happened. I simply knew it was inhuman and wrong.

"I'm good," I whispered as I got shakily to my feet. "I need a toothbrush and some toothpaste. Now."

"Here you go, baby," Mac said, helping me brush the awful taste out of my mouth. "You amaze me, Zelda—your power, your compassion. I'm humbled by everything that you are and I thank the Goddess you're mine."

"I wanted to play *Princess and the Penis* at the hotel," I whispered with a weak smile. "Not sure that's gonna happen."

Mac's delighted laugh want all through me and my weak smile grew a little wider.

"You did not just say *Princess and the Penis*," he said, still laughing.

"I most certainly did," I shot back as I leaned against him and breathed him in. "It would have been so awesome."

"I'm sure it would have been and don't count the fairytale out just yet, my witch," he said with a wink. "But I think we need to check on your patient first."

"Shit," I said, smacking myself in the head and then wincing. I'd been whacked enough for one day. I didn't need to add to it. "Let's go."

Zorro was a new man. He was beautiful before, but now he was redonkulous. His purple leather suit was back on and he was moving around without agonizing pain for the first time in I didn't even know how long. Tears streamed from his eyes and for the second time in an hour, he went to his knees.

"I am in your debt, Zelda," he whispered reverently. "You are a miracle."

"Nope," I said with a relieved grin that he was fixed. "I'm a materialistic, profane witch who got saddled with healing furballs. Get up, dude. You're making me itchy."

"As you wish, gurlfriend," Zorro said with a grin. "We shall see you at the witching hour?"

"Yep. Make sure Zach is there," I replied, leaning back on Mac again. I was going to have to take a long nap this afternoon or there was no way I could stay awake until midnight. Repairing someone's entire system of internal organs could tire a girl out.

"Zach will be there," Willow promised, bowing to me as well.

Willow wrapped her arms around a beaming Zorro and they disappeared in a pine-scented breeze and a pop of green sparkles.

"Well, it's a good thing I only blew up the living room of the suite," I commented as I took Mac's hand and headed for the bedroom... to sleep. "It would have sucked to sleep on the floor."

And then I slept like the dead.

I was bone-tired, but I was proud of myself. I was becoming a beautiful witch inside and out. It sure as fuck wasn't easy, but it felt very, very, *very* good.

CHAPTER TWELVE

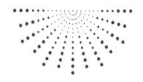

"Did you know that a pig orgasms for thirty minutes?" Sassy asked as we trudged through the woods looking for the X.

No one said anything because there wasn't much to say. The map Zorro had given us was vague and we were all frustrated. I could feel the magic in the air, but it was elusive and strange. However, I did feel safe in the woods surrounded by the magnificent towering trees. I wondered briefly if I could call to the trees, but my BFF's incessant yacking made it hard to think. Sassy had been educating us for the last thirty minutes with information she'd learned on Animal Planet. At this rate, I was going to disconnect her cable when we got home. Only Jeeves appeared interested and proud of the mostly gag-inducing facts his mate was spewing.

"A cockroach can live for nine days without its head before it starves to death," she pointed out as she ran smack dab into an enormous tree. "Dang it. That smarts."

"Youse is kiddin' me," Fat Bastard said as he, Jango Fett and Boba Fett appeared in a blast silver magic and smoke. "I wanna be a fuckin' pig."

I screamed. Sassy jumped so high she ran right back into the tree. Mac swore and Jeeves just laughed.

"Where have you fat asses been and how did you find us?" I demanded, with my hand over my rapidly beating heart. We were in the middle of thick woods about an hour outside of Lexington. I was pretty sure the dorks could track me, but I usually heard them coming.

"So youse decided to be a *girl* again?" Fat Bastard inquired accusingly, as he settled his porcine ass on a bed of pine needles and lifted his leg high in preparation for a nad lick.

"What are you talking about?" I snapped as I waved my hand and dressed his bottom half in a cement diaper so he couldn't get to his giggle berries.

"When youse ignored us and pretended youse didn't know who we was, weese figured dat was a sign," Boba Fett explained as he gave me a pissy glare.

"A sign for what?" I asked, not following the story or their reasoning. Not that I ever could truly follow what was going on in their warped kitty minds.

Jango just hissed. Apparently, he wasn't speaking to me. WTF?

"You dumbasses better tell me what's going on right now," I told them. "I have a lot of shit on my plate and I have no time for cryptic crap."

"Zelda is speaking German," Sassy told my pissed off cats. "She didn't really mean shit on a plate. However, since we were at a poop convention this morning, she could have meant shit on a plate—which would be all kinds of fucking gross. But the shit—shit being a Canadian word…"

"Youse said Zelda was speaking German," Fat Bastard said, perplexed.

"She was," Sassy said with an eye roll. "German and Canadian are practically the same. It's easy to get the accents confused.

Anyhoo, the *shit* that's not literal *shit* is that Zelda has a twin brother with a mother who drinks blood who is not *her* mother—which makes the twin thing slightly confusing to me. But since everyone else seems cool with that, I'm gonna guess they were speaking Swedish. Not to mention we found a gay goat shifter named Zorro who smokes menthol cigarettes with his butthole. Ohhh, and then there's Willow who promised me a new dress if I didn't set myself on fire. Also, polar bears are left-handed and lions have been known to bump fuzzies fifty times in one day."

"I'm a little baffled here," Jango stated, scratching his kitty head and trying to figure out if Sassy's diatribe had imparted anything useful.

"I'm not. Maybe bein' a lion would be better dan bein' a pig," Boba said thoughtfully.

"Lions are cats, youse douchebag," Fat Bastard said, whacking Boba in the back of his furry head. "If dey can get some stanky on the hang down fifty times a day, weese can too."

I almost puked in my mouth, but I had more important stuff to deal with right now. "Back to my original question. Where have you been?"

"Youse gots a twin?" the Bastard asked, narrowing his eyes at me.

"Possibly," I told him.

"Well, dats certainly some farked up news. Also explains why youse pretended not to know us," he said, as he struggled to get to his feet but collapsed under the weight of his cement diaper.

The facts supporting Zach actually being my twin kept increasing. My own familiars thought that he was me? Unreal.

"Oh shit," Jango choked out.

"What?" I demanded. It was almost midnight and we hadn't found the X yet. If we missed meeting up with Zorro,

Willow and Zach it would suck tremendously. My damn cats needed to get to the point. Fast.

"Umm..." Jango mumbled, not making eye contact. "Weese might have been mad dat youse ignored us."

"I didn't," I told them.

"Weese know dat *now*," Fat Bastard said, also not making eye contact. "But weese don't like bein' ignored."

"Oh my Goddess, what did you buttwads do?" I asked.

They exchanged glances and then shrugged in unison. Their unofficial idiot leader, Fat Bastard cleared his throat.

"Weese might have done a little tiny bit of graffiti work," he admitted.

"How little?" I shot back, not liking the sound of this.

"Well, weese might have enhanced Rump Arena with a few cuss words," Fat Bastard muttered.

"All of it?" I shouted. Rupp Arena was fucking enormous—it covered at least three city blocks.

"No, dollface," Fat Bastard said.

I sighed in relief. My freakin' cats were train wrecks.

"Only three sides," Jango said.

My freakin' cats were about to be *dead* train wrecks.

I inhaled through my nose and exhaled through my mouth. My cats grew wildly uncomfortable. They didn't like it when I stayed calm... and they shouldn't...

"Instead of tying you together by your tails and hurling you like a furry Frisbee into the great beyond, you're gonna take your misdemeanor loving sphincters back to Rupp Arena. The three of you are going to paint the entire building. *Tonight*. If even one profanity is left on the walls in the morning, you will be licking it off. You feel me?" I ground out.

"But weese only defaced three sides," Boba pointed out.

"Unless you can get paint to match the clean side, you will paint the whole fucking thing," I snapped.

"Youse is a hard woman, dollface," Fat bastard said with a grin.

"Thank you. I think this is a mature way to handle it," I replied. "My first instinct was to shave you bald, take pictures and put them on the internet."

"I'd wax them," Sassy said. "If you shave them, you'll get hair all over your fabu dress. With the wax, the fur will come off in bloody clumps. Waxing ensures there won't be a bunch of excess hair floating around. I could film you doing it with my phone and we could send it to Animal Planet."

"And on dat note, we're outta here," Fat Bastard said, smacking his little kitty paws together as the three of them vanished in a puff of smoke.

They'd been waxed by Sassy not too long ago for firing her chipmunk sons and had sequestered themselves for weeks after that. There was no way in hell my cats were going to hang out and see if Sassy was for real.

"You do realize your familiar is still wearing a cement diaper," Mac commented with a chuckle.

"Not my problem," I shot back with a grin. "We need to find the X."

"You've found it," Zach said as he stepped out of the shadows and took in our group.

"Where are Willow and Zorro?" I asked, watching him warily.

He wasn't exactly happy to see me, but he didn't seem like he was as angry either.

"Right here, gurlfriend," Zorro said, dropping down from the branch of a tree.

"And Willow?" I looked up to see if she was about to drop in as well.

"Right here," Willow said as she disengaged herself from the trunk of the tree I was standing next to. Or at least I thought she did.

I rubbed my hands over my eyes. I had to be seeing things. Maybe I'd needed a longer nap. Healing Zorro had almost wrecked me. Willow's arrival was the strangest thing I'd ever witnessed.

"Umm... you have a twig in your hair," I said as reached over and pulled it out.

Willow winced as it detached from her head and broke off in my hand. Quickly handing the twig back to her, I felt horrible. I was pretty sure what I'd just done equated to ripping hair out of her head. She smiled and placed the leafy stick back on her head where it promptly reattached itself. WTF? I mean I was a freakin' witch mated to a man who turned into a wolf. Why was any of this odd to me?

"So... umm... You're a tree?" I asked.

Willow shook her head and giggled. "Nope."

"Could have sworn you just walked out of a tree," I told her.

"Kind of," she agreed.

"It's just a trick," Zach said, growing impatient.

Willow sighed sadly and shook her chin fell. Clearly, it wasn't *just a trick*. Zach was too wrapped up in his own hell to bother to figure out the woman who adored him. I understood this all too well. However, I still didn't know what Willow was.

"I haven't much time," Zach said flatly. "Who are these people with you? Can they be trusted?"

"We can be trusted," Mac said coolly, staring at Zach in shock. "I'm Zelda's mate, Mac. And this is my son, Jeeves. We're all family."

Jeeves was equally as surprised at how identical Zach and I were. It still freaked me out. And it definitely freaked Zach out.

"Thank you for healing Zorro," Zach said begrudgingly. "As I'm never at full power, I haven't been able to truly take care of him."

"I didn't do it for you," I said flatly. "I did it for him."

"Whatever your reason, I'm grateful."

I nodded and tried to spot traces of the spell cast on him lingering around his aura. Nothing. Shit. That meant it was intricate or cast by a species I wasn't familiar with.

"We have to touch each other," I said, slowly approaching him and feeling more whole with each step.

"Why?" Zach asked as he too felt the pull.

"One, because I need to feel for the spell and see if I can break it."

I took two more steps forward. He did too.

"And two?" he asked, looking ashen and pained.

"Because I need to," I whispered, now face to face with him. I didn't dare initiate. I waited for my brother to touch me first.

"Will this work?" Zach asked tersely.

He searched my face looking for something. Himself? I knew that's what I was looking for in his eyes.

"I have no fucking idea if it will work, but since the moment I saw you I wanted to touch you. Did you feel the same draw?"

"I did," he admitted though it seemed to frustrate him.

"On three?" I asked.

His nod was curt and his hand shook as he raised it to mine. My skin felt too tight on my body and my breathing came out in short bursts. As our fingertips met, a gust of light golden magic exploded around us. Closing my eyes, I felt the tears leak out and roll down my cheeks. I tasted the salty drops and knew this was just the beginning of the pain we needed to feel so we had a chance to heal… together. I wrapped my arms around the person I should have had by my side for the last thirty-one years.

Zach held me tight and pressed his forehead to mine. His memories became tangled with my own and I gasped at how degrading and horrifying his life had been. Placing my hands on either side of his face, I tried to absorb his pain. However, my twin was doing the same. The devastation I experienced seeing his past fly across my vision was tempered as he tried to absorb the pain of my childhood.

His touch was full of love. My touch told the same story. The love we had for each other was clear, true and simple—the love that had been stolen from us by a woman so heinous there weren't enough words to make it make sense.

"I can't find the spell," I whispered raggedly. "Where is it?"

"I have no memory of it," he said. "I was a baby."

"I can find it," Sassy said, stepping forward. "If you trust me."

"How?" Zach asked, glancing over at my insane BFF.

"I can go into your mind and search your memories," she replied.

"Nope. No way," I said without missing a beat. "I can't take that risk. I just found Zach."

Jeeves stepped forward and gently touched my back. "Sassy is an expert now. She has practiced on me, her father, and Marge daily for the last two months. Marge insisted that she become a master at mind diving... and now I think I know why."

"Fuck Baba Yaga and Cookie Witch," I muttered still hanging onto Zach as if my life depended on it. "They probably knew all about this."

"I don't think so," Mac said, coming to my side and placing his hands on both Zach and me. "I didn't know that the pack in Lexington had scattered and were being systematically eliminated. Even though magic is everywhere, the details are not always evident. I can say with great confidence that Baba Yaga would not have let this continue to happen if she had known."

"Gurlfriend, can I cut in here?" Zorro inquired.

"Sure," I replied.

"The one thing Henrietta's power can do is mask what is happening around her—it's a dark power," Zorro explained, shuddering. "She claims to be able to kill with a touch, but I've never seen that happen. I think it's a lie."

"It's not," Willow said with a catch in her voice. "It's not a lie."

Zach said nothing, but his jaw worked a mile a minute.

We all mulled the awful nugget of info in silence for a bit. Henrietta Smith had to be done away with, but if that meant killing my brother it was out of the question. However, if I could break the spell…

"Sassy? If you can swear on Witch's Honor you won't hurt my brother, I want you to do it. I need you to find the spell in his memories. Or maybe the spell is in my memory too," I said, getting excited. "Go into my head and see if I have it. Then we don't have to touch Zach."

"Absolutely not," Zach snapped, pulling away from me. "None of this is a good idea. If there's a chance of it going wrong, your friend will harm me—not you. If I die, my *mother* dies. I will go on to the Next Adventure knowing I did something worthy with my life."

"I don't like that," I snapped as my fingers began to spark.

"Do I look like I care?" Zach snapped right back.

"Actually you do, dick," I said with a raised brow.

"Maybe I do, asshole," he shot back with a small smile on his lips. "But what I say goes here. My life means far less than yours. If someone dies tonight, it will be me. Goddess knows it will be a relief."

Willow's muffled cry didn't go unnoticed by me, but Zach seemed not to hear it.

"I'm ready," he said to Sassy. "Please avoid my other memories if possible. I wouldn't want to put that on any living being."

Sassy nodded. Putting down her broom, she centered herself and slowly approached Zach. Gone was the flighty idiot and in her place was a powerful, beautiful witch. Her blonde hair floated around her head and her skin glowed. Placing her hands on my brother's temples, she leaned in and kissed his forehead.

"Relax, Zach," she whispered in a voice full of confidence and love. "Let me in."

The enchantment that floated through the forest was golden in color and laced with hints of pink. It tickled my nose and calmed my soul. Zach closed his eyes as Sassy wandered around his memories. She was as still as if she was in a trance and her brow was wrinkled in deep thought.

As quickly as she'd gone in, she came out.

"Are you okay, Zach?" she asked in a strangled whisper that made me feel like crying. "Would you like me to go back in and take the nightmares away?"

"No," Zach said firmly and with little emotion. "I own my past. I will keep it no matter how ugly."

"As you wish," she said as she stepped away from Zach. "You guys were really cute babies. Zach *is* your twin. Both your mother and Henrietta were there when the spell was cast. But neither of you saw it. You were napping. I could feel the presence of both women and I could feel Zach's chemistry change... but that's all."

"You saw us together?" I whispered, not trying to hold back my anger or my tears any longer.

Sassy nodded and then pressed her face into Jeeves chest.

"What else did you see?" I asked.

"I don't want my memories shared," Zach ground out. "Ever."

"I won't. I promise," Sassy said.

"But what about us—us together? Did you see any more of us as babies together?" I pressed. "How long were we with each other?"

Sassy turned to me. She was pale and her eyes were watery. "A day. You were only together a day... and then she sold him."

"*Motherfucker*," I shouted as I turned and blew a crater in the forest floor as big as an SUV.

The trees bent forward and their branches reached out to comfort me. I heard Willow gasp in surprise, but I didn't have time to explain that I was buddies with all the trees in the world. I was still coming to terms with that one myself.

Wrapping my hand around a low hanging branch, I let the magic calm me. "I have to go pay someone a visit. Alone."

"Not alone. I'm coming with you," Zach corrected me.

"Dude, this is not a reunion of any kind," I hissed at him. "I'm just gonna lay this shit out so you can understand. Our mother freakin' *sold* you. She's beyond despicable and you've been through enough. This is *mine*. I won't let her near you ever in this lifetime—she doesn't deserve you. You feel me? *Judith,* or whatever the hell she's going by now, is not what you might have daydreamed she was your whole life. She tried to kill me for my magic—she's incapable of love and it took me almost thirty years and some frightening fucking therapy with a porno-loving rabbit Shifter to realize I was lovable." I took a breath. "Actually, it started with the musical version of *Mommie Dearest*. That was the impetus—but that's a story for another day."

A small and perplexed smile pulled at Zach's lips. "Did you actually just say the musical version of *Mommie Dearest?*"

"Yep. I did," I replied, realizing how insane I sounded. I wanted my brother to like me, not think I was batshit crazy. But if the shoe fit…

"*Mommie Dearest* is a musical?" Zach asked, still trying to digest the alarming news.

"Yes. Sadly, yes," I told him with a small giggle. "It sucked."

"Not so fast, dude. I was Christina and I was amazeballs," Sassy chimed in, back to her old self.

"She was," I agreed with an eye roll. "It was directed by our father, Fabio."

"Stop, Zelda," Zach growled. "I have no mother or father. It's hard enough to accept you, but I'm going to try."

"Fabio didn't know about me," I said quickly as Zach began to glow. "If he didn't know about me, then he didn't know about you either."

Zach sighed. I caught a brief hint of desperate longing in his green eyes that were so like mine, but it was gone just as quickly as it came.

"No, Zelda," he said flatly. "I'll accept that I have you, but no more. However, if the spell can't be broken, I need your promise that you will leave me here and never come back."

"Fine," I lied through my teeth.

"Witch's Honor," Zach said, obviously seeing right through me.

What to do…

If I made a silent deal with the Goddess and she was aware I was lying, I wondered if she would zap my ass clean off my body for breaking the sacred Witch's Honor. Honestly, I didn't care. While my ass was outstanding, my brother meant more to me.

Oh. My. Hell. What was happening? Was I so nice that I was going to live with no ass? Yes. Yes, I was.

"Witch's Honor," I said, putting one hand behind me and crossing my fingers.

Zach nodded, but I could tell he wasn't sure if he believed me. Whatever. Now that I found him, he was mine and I was keeping him—forever.

"Jeeves and I will go back to Lexington. I want to help relocate the Shifters that are still here," Mac said, kissing the top of my head.

"How many are left?" I asked, hugging him tight.

"Only five," he replied with an expression of disgust. "I'm going to send them to Assjacket. They need to feel safe."

"I love you," I told him, not wanting to let him go.

"Love you more, little witch," he replied with a smile that made my heart feel light.

"I'll go with Jeeves and Mac unless you need me," Sassy said, laying her head on my shoulder and then kissing my cheek. "I can poof the Shifters to Assjacket if they're ready to go."

"Go with Mac and Jeeves. The next part of the journey is mine… and Zach's. Just give Baba Yaga and Fabio a heads up if you're gonna send unfamiliar Shifters to town," I told her. "And make sure Bob the beaver isn't on the welcoming committee. If they think everyone has a fucking unibrow, they might not want to stay."

"Good plan," Sassy said with a thumbs up.

Turning my attention to a very quiet Zorro and Willow, I smiled. "We're kind of freaky," I acknowledged.

"Umm… I'd have to disagree, gurlfriend," Zorro said with a wide grin. "I'd have to say you're all kinds of awesome."

"I second that," Willow added.

I was very cognizant that Willow wanted to go to Zach, but his body language didn't welcome it. Instead, she stood next to Zorro and held his hand.

"We'll stay close by and monitor if Henrietta wakes," Zorro said.

Zach swore under his breath and a sharp angry wind whipped through the woods. "You will stay away from her if she wakes. Do you both understand me?"

Willow and Zorro nodded.

"Wait. How will we reach you if we need you or you need us?" I asked Zorro and Willow as the stick wand in my pocket began to vibrate. WTH? Yanking it out of my pocket, I stared at the sparkling twig.

"Use that," Willow said with a small giggle. "I will come when called and I can send you a message through it too."

"You're sure you're not a fucking tree?" I asked, looking at the gorgeous woman askance.

"Not a fucking tree," she said.

"You wouldn't lie to me?"

"Nope," she said with another giggle. "I wood…ent."

The trees in the forest shook with what I could only guess was laughter at Willow's corny tree joke. Clearly, Willow had tree buddies too.

"Dawn will come in a few hours and I have to be back," Zach said, pulling my attention away from the need to play fifty questions with Willow. She might not be a tree, but I was on the right track.

"You ready?" I asked my brother.

"I was born ready," he replied with a smirk, using a line I always used.

Standing here staring at my brother was both perfect and terrifying. Perfect because we'd finally found each other. Terrifying… because I wasn't sure how long it would last.

CHAPTER THIRTEEN

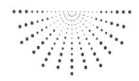

"She's in there?" Zach asked, eyeing the building only two hundred away feet from where we were standing.

His body language was tense and his complexion was pale. This had to be surreal for him. It was bizarre to me, but I couldn't begin to imagine what my brother was thinking. He was about to meet the woman who had given birth to him and then sold him.

I would have been okay with never seeing my mother again, but this wasn't about me. It was about saving my brother, which, in turn, was about me I suppose. The bond was already there. I could feel Zach inside of my heart.

"Yep. She's in there," I said, experiencing the same sick feeling in my stomach I'd felt most of my life when dealing with my mother.

I'd thought I'd left any emotion for the woman behind, but the trembling of my hands proved differently. Shit.

"Who are the short, angry looking warlocks guarding the door?" Zach whispered.

We were hidden behind a large oak tree across the street from the place that still gave me the chills. Touching the bark of the tree calmed me and I smiled. I laid my cheek against it and sighed. The wand that my tree minions had given me warmed up in my pocket.

"Warren and Herb," I whispered. "They're part of Baba Yaga's spooky posse of weird ass, bobble-headed warlock minions. And just so you know, they're not real fond of me."

Zach chuckled. "You wanna explain why?"

"Nope."

"Roger that," he replied and then tried again. "You sure? It might be good to know if I have to save your ass."

This was not going to make my brother like me much, but he should know the extent of Warren and Herm's dislike. I'd earned it, but so had they. "Suffice it to say they didn't like having vaginas."

Zach shook his head and tried not to laugh. He failed. It hadn't been one of my finer moments, but then again I'd had many of those.

"Remind me to stay on your good side," Zach muttered, still shaking his head in disbelief.

"Look, the ugly turd knockers called Sassy stupid and worthless in front of a lot of people. It made her cry and then blow up my new car. Sassy might be an idiot, but she's *my* idiot, and I loved that car. Her self-esteem isn't great to start with and she certainly doesn't need assholes who come up to her knee making her feel horrible about herself. No one is allowed to smack talk my imbecile BFF."

Zach stared at me with an expression I couldn't decipher. Shit. He probably didn't like me either... or he thought I was nuts. Actually, I was nuts. But I still wanted him to like me and even love me eventually.

"When was this?" he asked with the tiniest hint of a smile on his full lips.

"Last week," I replied and scrunched my nose.

"So no chance they might have forgotten about it?" Zach inquired, now grinning.

"Umm… I'm gonna go with a no on that one," I told him, grinning back.

We'd poofed to Salem, Massachusetts. The pokey for witches was housed in a hotel from the early 1900s. It had converted to a magical prison about a hundred years ago.

From the outside, the decrepit building was glamoured to look like a charming bed and breakfast, complete with climbing ivy and flowers growing out of every conceivable nook and cranny. Inside it was cold and ugly with barren brick walls covered with Goddess knew what kind of slime. It was heavily warded with magic, keeping all mortals and responsible magic-makers away. It was run by a humor-free staff of witches and warlocks… all older than dirt.

Just looking at it brought back the memories of my old home away from home—cell block D. It was the wing designated for witches who abused their magic as easily as they changed their underwear. My guess was that my mother wasn't in cell block D. Nope. She wasn't even a witch anymore.

"Before we enter what I assume will be hell," Zach said, running his hands through his hair. "Can you explain how the woman who bore us used to be a witch and is now a human?"

"Umm… sure," I told him, trying to figure out how to truncate the very long and involved horror story. "Judith was in cahoots with vicious honey badgers who were fucking with the magical balance *and* trying to unseat the Baba Yaga *and* take over the Universe. She tried to kill me and take my power. But first she had our Aunt Hildy murdered. Of course, the fucking honey badgers turned on our sorry excuse of a mother and stole Aunt Hildy's magic for themselves. Soooo, long story short, I punched my fist into the honey badger's chest and took back our Aunt Hildy's magic. Then when dear old mom tried to off my ass, I punched my fist into her chest and took her magic. The suck ass part of that is that she had dark magic inside her... and now I do too."

Zach looked a little green as he listened. "So you like to punch your fist into people's chests?"

"Fuck no. It was gross," I said with a gag. "I didn't have the heart to kill her even though she'd done her best to kill me, so I did the next best thing I could do. I made her human."

"I would have killed her," Zach said flatly.

I was silent for a long moment. Was that why he'd wanted to come with me? Was he going to kill Judith? As much as the thought satisfied some very dark part inside of me, it wasn't going to happen on my watch.

"Living as a human is more of a punishment than death for a witch," I told Zach, watching for his reaction.

"I'd have to disagree," he shot back. "Living as a warlock sold to a human is a punishment worse than death."

I had nothing to say to that. I was going to have no part of this, but after seeing inside Zach's thoughts, I couldn't blame him for wanting to end our mother.

"It won't make you feel good," I said softly. "I had the chance to do it and I couldn't. A stupid ass part of me was still hoping she would love me."

"Love is a myth," Zach said. "It doesn't exist."

I wanted to whack him in the head. I already loved him and I'd known him only a day. Since I was pretty sure he'd whack me back with a zap of magic if I nailed him, I shoved my hands into the pockets of my awesome dress. My brother had no reason to believe in love... or did he?

"Zorro loves you," I said.

"He's indebted to me for saving his life."

"I call bullshit, *brother*."

"You can call whatever you want, *sister*," Zach said with a shrug.

"Willow loves you," I pointed out carefully as the stick in

my pocket warmed again. Willow had to be a freakin' tree... or a tree something. "And you're a dumbass for not seeing that."

"Tell me something I don't know," he said in a harsh tone. Zach closed his eyes and his lips compressed into a straight line. "Willow is foolish. I'm not worthy of such feelings from any living thing."

His absolute conviction of his worthlessness and self-hatred made my heart ache. Zach was my new mission. And I didn't need him to start off what I hoped would be his new life by killing our egg donor.

"Listen to me," I said, getting up in his face. "We need our shitty excuse of a mother to tell us how to reverse the spell. She has to be kind of alive to do that. You feel me?"

"What exactly do you mean by *kind of*?"

"Misspeak on my part," I said with an eye roll. "Don't kill her."

"Is that an order?" Zach inquired as his eyes narrowed dangerously. "Will you punch me in the chest and remove my magic if I disobey?"

"Okay, that's really fucking gross," I snapped, giving him a glare that usually made people run for cover. He didn't. "I'm not taking anything from you. Enough has already been taken from both of us. I'm just telling you—and I know I'm right because of the shit loads of therapy I've had with a rabbit who likes porn—that killing her won't make you happy or solve anything."

Zach raised a brow and stared at me. It truly was like looking in a mirror except he was a dude. I wasn't sure if the raised brow was in judgment that I went to a therapist who liked smutty movies and magazines or if it was because he had no clue that he'd feel bad about offing our mother.

"Look, it might feel great in the moment to end her, but in the long run it will suck." I tried reasoning with him. I considered offering him candy since it worked with my kids, but thought better of it.

"You don't know me, Zelda. I'm not a good person," he said darkly.

"And neither am I, so we're a perfect fit."

"No," he said, putting his hand on my cheek and smiling sadly. "You're good and pretend not to be."

Zach nailed me, but I could also nail him. No one as awful as he thought he was would have taken a near dead goat Shifter under his protection and continued to care for him.

"You're full of shit," I informed him. "You're me a few years ago. I'm gonna fix your sorry ass or die trying."

"My ass is fantastic. It doesn't need fixing," he said with a small lopsided grin. "And if we don't reverse the spell, we will never see each other again after today."

"Then I suggest we reverse the fucking spell, douchebag."

"Nothing would make me happier, dorkass," he replied. "Are you ready?"

"Nope, but that hasn't stopped me yet," I said grabbing his hand in mine. "Let's do this shit."

CHAPTER FOURTEEN

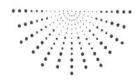

"If you don't have an appointment or aren't here to be incarcerated you can't enter," Warren said, his beady little eyes dancing with psychotic delight.

It was obvious the bastard was happy to deny me. However, he wasn't going to be happy shortly. I did notice that both he and Herm had stepped behind large cement planters to hide their privates.

"Assface," I said sweetly as he squinted at me and tried to figure out if he'd heard me correctly. "I'm going in and so is my brother."

"No," Herb said with a scowl. "You are not."

I sighed dramatically. "Okay, then we'll just hang out with you buttbags until I can get Baba Yoharshpunishment up here and tattle on you for not letting the future Baba Yaga in."

"You wish," Herm hissed. "Carol isn't retiring any time soon. And you aren't fit to shine my shoes, witch."

"I sure as hell hope not," I told him. "My magic is still seriously iffy—hence the hoohas you two were sporting last week. Lemme practice on you. Cool?" I inquired as I waved my hand and gave Herm a pink Mohawk, much to his horror.

"Stop that," Herm snapped. "You will not like my retaliation. I can destroy you. And I will do so with pleasure."

Goddess, I was grateful for my dorky tree minions. I'd take a corny tree joke over this bullshit any day of the week. The little bastards that served the Baba Yaga were miniature nightmares with seriously bad attitudes.

"Duuuuuuude, I don't like your tone of voice," I ground out, clapping my hands and giving them each a large set of double D's and uni-brows. "Do not fuck with me. I'm a little on edge at the moment and that doesn't bode well for your tiny testicles. You feel me?"

"Undo this," Warren snarled, starting to glow. "You are a menace and a blight on all Witchdom. We have plans to stop your ascension when the time comes. And it won't be pleasant—for you."

"*No one* is going to stop me from taking a job I don't want—especially someone with elephant ears and duck feet," I snarled right back at him.

"I don't have elephant ears and duck feet," Herm growled.

"Whoops, hang on," I said waving my hand and making my statement come true. "Now you do. And just so we're clear here. The spell can only be reversed by me. Baba Yodummy can't help you."

"You are wretched," Warren grunted as he tripped over his ears and landed on Herm. "One day you shall pay dearly."

"*Not* today," I said, stepping over them and opening the front door.

Zach didn't step over the hissing and spitting warlocks. He stepped right on them. "Do not fuck with my sister. She's being nice. If you talk to her like that again, you will deal with me. I'm not nice," he said as the warlocks cowered in fear.

Zach's defense of me made giddy. He liked me.

"Are you going to leave them like that?" he asked as he followed me inside.

"No, I'll reverse the spell when we're done here. But I am going to have a sit down with Baba Yaga about her icky minions wanting to end me."

"Do you have icky warlock minions?"

"Goddess in drop crotch pants, no," I said. "I have freaky trees as minions and three nut licking cats as familiars."

"Trees?" he asked.

"Yep. Sponge Bob, Sleepy, Doc, Sneezy and Grumpy."

"Well, that makes sense," Zach said.

"How in the hell does that make sense to you? I'm still kinda put out about it. Those big bastards are freakin' destructive."

"It makes sense why Willow is so obsessed with you."

"Not following," I replied in a cranky tone. "Do you know what Willow is too?"

He nodded and closed his eyes for a moment. "I do even though she thinks I don't."

Zach opened his eyes and we stared at each other. The pain in his expression made me want to hug him, but his body language made it clear that my affection wasn't welcome.

"She loves you."

"I know," he said, sounding defeated. "It's better that she believes I don't care."

"But you do?" I asked.

Zach's face turned completely expressionless—like there was no one home inside him.

"Zelda, I have nothing to offer anyone—even you—and definitely not Willow. I'm tied to a snake whose only concern is living forever. It's selfish of me to even keep Zorro and Willow around. If we can reverse the spell, then maybe things can be different. If we can't, I want something from you."

"What?" I asked as my chest tightened and my heart began to beat faster.

"You think you love me... right?"

"I know I do," I told him, unembarrassed and unashamed.

"Then will you promise me something?" he asked.

"Depends on what it is." I knew this wasn't going to be good, but I would hear him out.

"If we can't break the spell, I want you to kill me," he stated as benignly as if he was talking about the weather.

I was stunned to silence. There was no way on the Goddesses green earth that I could take my brother's life. It would be like taking my own.

"The spell prohibits me from killing myself," Zach explained. "Goddess knows I've tried so many times I can't count. Henrietta kills to live and I have to take some responsibility for that."

"No one is responsible for what other people do," I said as my eyes filled with tears.

"I can't stop her," Zach said harshly. "I've watched her do it and I did nothing."

I didn't believe that for a second. "The spell prevents you from stopping her?" I whispered, sick at what he'd seen and had to go through.

Zach nodded his affirmation in a jerky motion. "It doesn't matter. I'm part of the vicious cycle. It has to end and you can help me end it."

I understood and I didn't. I'd been through my own personal hell, but it wasn't nearly as bad as my brother's. Already I would do just about anything for him... except end him.

"How about this?" I said, sucking my bottom lip into my mouth. "Let's try to undo the spell first and then revisit this conversation if we have to. Fair?"

"Fair," Zach said as he blew out a relieved breath. "You're a good sister."

His requirements for a good sister were a bit alarming, but I didn't blame him for it. In his shoes, I would have probably begged for the same thing.

"Let's go have a little chat with our egg donor," I said, very ready to change the subject.

"Lead the way, sister. I'm your right hand man."

And that was how I wanted it to stay. Forever.

CHAPTER FIFTEEN

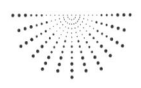

"Do you know where she is?" Zach inquired as we walked down hallway after hallway with no results.

"Of course, I do," I said with a monster eye roll. "I just thought we should get some exercise before we dropped in for a visit."

Zach laughed. I didn't. The pokey was a whole lot larger than I remembered. However, I'd spent my entire time in a cell so what the hell did I know?

"Take my hands," Zach instructed. "You know what she looks like, correct?"

I nodded and took his hands. "You can find her because I know what she looks like?"

Zach just smiled and led us to a wooden wall. "Lean on the wood. I need to pull the energy from it to see clearly."

"Where'd you learn this?" I asked as I did as I was told.

"Willow," he said.

Holy Goddess in black socks and sandals, the clues were starting making sense. The only problem was, I was pretty sure that the conclusion I'd come to didn't exist.

"So Willow pulls power from trees?"

"She does," he said, eyeing me with amusement. "You figured it out yet?"

"Maybe. I wasn't seeing things when she walked out of the trunk of the tree?"

"Nope," Zach said as bright shimmering green sparkles began to pop around his head like a halo making him look like an angel.

"And the twig I pulled off her head was really connected?" I asked.

"It was."

"Shit," I said with a wince. "That couldn't have felt good."

"I need you to concentrate on the egg donor's face," Zach instructed and closed his eyes.

"I will in a sec," I promised. "Is Willow a bagworm Shifter?"

Zach's eyes popped open and his grin was wide. "Do not *ever* let her hear you say that. She would have a shit fit." His brow wrinkled in confusion. "Is bagworm Shifter even a real thing?

"It was a shitty guess," I shot back defensively. "And I have no clue if they exist. The only other things I can think of *really* don't exist. They're only in fairy tales."

Zach stared at me dumbfounded. "Witches are in fairy tales. Do you believe they exist?"

"Umm... duh," I said, thinking there might be a lot I didn't know.

"Fairy tale creatures exist. Mostly they're awful."

I rolled my eyes. I wasn't falling for that shit. "Mmmkay, whatever you say."

Zach rolled his eyes and beat my eye roll, which sucked so I rolled my eyes again.

"Are we having a contest here?" he inquired with a grin as he rolled his eyes once again... and fucking won.

"So trolls exist?" I asked, holding back an eye roll that in no way could beat his. I did not like to lose.

"Yep," he said. "Very smelly."

Willow couldn't be a troll. She smelled great. "Hint?"

"No can do, sis. I don't like getting zapped by the Goddess of *nature*."

"Did you just give me a hint?" I asked, getting frustrated.

"Maybe."

Nature... not a witch... gets power from trees... not a fucking bagworm Shifter... gives great eye roll... dresses like a fashion model... fairy tale creature.

"What was your favorite subject in school?" Zach asked, leaning against the wall and realizing I wasn't going to give up.

"Lunch."

"Umm... okay. Did you take mythology?"

"Nope."

Zach sighed and ran his hand through his hair. "You're a pain in the ass."

"Thank you," I replied. "If we play a hint game that wouldn't be cheating, right?"

"Since we're wasting time here, I'll play your game—for two minutes. When you're not wet you're...?"

Shit. I was horrible at games. Why in the hell had I suggested a fucking game? Henry and Audrey beat me regularly at Candy Land... even when I cheated. "Lightly perspiring?" I guessed. Wrong—if the look on Zach's face was any indication.

"No. Another way to say arid is..."

"Hot."

"No. Two syllables. Second syllable. If you don't subtract you..." Zach hinted.

"You have more," I said triumphantly.

My brother's chin hit his chest and he groaned. "You get one more shot. And remind me never to be your partner in charades."

"Two more shots. There are two fucking syllables," I said

with a raised brow and middle finger. "And give me good ones."

"I have been," he muttered. "What rhymes with bad and starts with A?"

"Add," I shouted, feeling like I got that one correct.

"Yep," Zach said with a chuckle. "What rhymes with pry and starts with D?"

"Dry!" I said as I danced around, pumping my arms in the air. "Willow is an Adddry. And how any of you idiots thought I would figure that shit out, I will never know. Never even heard of an Adddry."

"I'm done so with you," Zach said and went to grab my hands again. "We can try this again later. After we find the egg donor."

"I didn't get it?" I asked, deflated.

"You didn't get it, but you will… maybe," he said with a smile. "You would have driven me insane if we'd grown up together."

"I know," I said with a giggle. "It would have been awesome."

That sobered both of us and reminded us why we were here. We didn't grow up together. We weren't able to protect each other from the horrors that had been our childhoods. And the person responsible for that was somewhere in the building.

Extending my hands to my brother, I closed my eyes and pictured my mother. I felt a zing go through my body as Zach's hands gripped mine tight. His breathing was choppy and I grew lightheaded as I felt him absorb the image of our mother from my mind.

"She's right around the corner," he said tightly, letting my hands drop. "We've passed her at least five times."

CHAPTER SIXTEEN

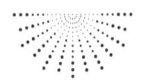

SHE DIDN'T EVEN TURN AROUND WHEN WE ENTERED. IT WAS IF WE didn't exist. However, that was the way it had always been. I'd been invisible to my mother my entire life.

"Put it on the table. I'll eat when I'm hungry. You can leave," she said dismissively.

Zach glanced at me and I shrugged. She clearly thought we were the hired help. She was wrong.

Judith was in a suite of sorts. It was far more posh than the cell I'd spent nine months in. It looked more like an upscale apartment. Maybe it was her home now—a home with guards and bars on the windows. I was surprised there were mirrors in the room, but then I remembered that my mother had no magical power anymore and couldn't scry.

"We're not room service," I said and realized my stupid voice was shaking.

Zach put his arm around me and pulled me close to his side. The connection to the person who was the other half of me calmed me and gave me strength.

Judith's shoulders tensed and she slowly turned her head. There was only the merest flicker of surprise in her still beautiful eyes as she took us in. It vanished as quickly as it had arrived. Our mother now just stared at us as if we were strangers who had wandered into her quarters.

"What do you want?" she asked coldly.

Zach's body was as tense as it could be without exploding—literally. I could feel that talking wasn't going to work for him. Not a problem, I had his back... and I always would from this day forward.

"This is your son, *mother*," I said flatly. "The son you sold into blood slavery."

Judith nodded and continued to stare at us blankly.

"You have *nothing* to say?" Zach ground out as his magic began to leak out causing a small fire on the rug we were standing on.

"What do you want me to say?" she inquired with disinterest as she watched the fire burn. "I liked that rug."

Waving my hand, I doused the fire. Not for her sake though. I thought it might be a bad idea to burn the pokey down. I'd already disfigured the asshole guards. Incinerating the building probably wouldn't go over well.

"How about an explanation? You owe us that much," I demanded, wanting to zap her ass or crawl over on my hands and knees and beg her to love me. My agonizing childish needs had not gone away. I realized they would probably never go away. My weakness infuriated me.

"What's to tell?" she asked, bored with the conversation that meant everything to Zach and me. "You've clearly figured it out. Male healers aren't as powerful. I had no use for a male."

"So you *sold* me?" Zach choked out, furious.

"It was either that or drown you," Judith said with a careless shrug. "I was being kind to let you exist."

My dark magic was so close to the surface, I could taste it. My arms and chest were now covered in a sparkling black enchantment. Zach glanced over at me and his eyes widened in shock.

"I told you I had dark magic," I hissed at him and tried to control my need to blow our egg donor to smithereens. I could literally feel my brother's heart shredding inside his chest. He never should have come here with me. These memories could never be erased.

"If you've come to end me, get it over with. If not, you're welcome to leave," Judith informed us picking up a book off the table and opening it up to read.

She hadn't moved a fraction of an inch closer to us. There was no instinct in Judith to touch or show any affection to the two people she'd given birth to. What had happened to her to make her like this? Hugging and loving Henry and Audrey was a no brainer to me—it was second nature.

"I have twins," I said, wondering if she would react to anything we said or did.

"You do?" Zach asked with a smile of surprised delight.

"I do," I told him with a grin, forgetting Judith was in the room for a moment. "Henry and Audrey—red curls and chubby cheeks. I miss them so much right now it hurts. They're gonna love you."

The expression in Zach's eyes was a mix of joy and pain. As far as my own twin was concerned, he believed there might be no tomorrow for him. That's when I was jerked back into our harsh reality. I remembered where we were and what we were doing.

"Tell me the spell you cast on Zach the day you sold him," I snapped, turning back to the unfeeling woman who watched us with barely restrained apathy.

Judith looked at me like I was stupid—not an unfamiliar expression for her. "I cast no spell on the boy."

"You gave the *boy* a name," I snarled, wondering what game she was playing. "Use it. The boy's name is *Zach*. You destroyed his life by selling him and casting a spell that ties him to a woman possibly worse than you—which is hard to fucking believe. So spill it, Judith. Tell me the spell you cast. Maybe then the Goddess will look more kindly on you on your reckoning day."

Her indifference made me furious. Her words made me want to end her before Zach did it.

"I told you," she said. "I cast no spell."

"Lies," I shouted. "Do you want to be taken out by the two people that you brought into this world?"

"It would certainly be a fitting end," Baba Yaga said as she poofed into the room in a blast of peach and silver glitter.

The Baba Yaga had arrived in all her eighties glory. It was clear that Zach had no clue who she was. I wanted to give him a heads up, but there was no time for that. He'd have to figure it out himself.

Judith wasn't any more interested in Carol's entrance than she was in her children's presence. She buried herself in her book and ignored all of us.

"My Goddess," Baba Yaga said as she stared at Zach as if she'd seen a ghost. "This is truly unbelievable."

I closed my eyes and thanked the Goddess. It was very clear that Baba Yaga knew nothing of my twin. Mac had been correct. This was a good thing because I would have torn Carol's ass to shreds if she'd known no matter how powerful she was.

"And you are?" Zach asked warily.

Baba Yaga was a bit taken aback by the question. Every witch and warlock in the Universe knew who she was. She continued to stare at the two of us and then smiled.

"I'm Baba Yaga—the caretaker of all witches and warlocks."

"You missed one," I said rudely.

"So I see," Baba replied.

She didn't smite me for my disrespect. I was positive she understood.

"And is having a brother the reason you turned two of my minions into circus freaks?" she questioned.

As she spoke, Baba Yaga crossed the room and removed the book from Judith's hands. When Judith began to protest, Baba flicked her fingers and burned the book to ash.

"Herb and Warren wouldn't let me in," I explained. "So I…"

"I did it," Zach said, not understanding the relationship between Baba Yaga and me. "Zelda did nothing. None of this was her idea. If a punishment is to be handed down, it belongs to me."

"Is that so?" Baba Yaga asked, squinting at the two of us.

"No," I said.

"Yes," Zach insisted, giving me a *shut your mouth* look.

Baba Yaga clapped her hands together and laughed. "Goddess, this is delightful."

Zach was confused, but I was used to her. However, since she was here… "Judith sold Zach as a baby and cast a spell on him tying his life to a fucking psycho. I need to know the spell so I can reverse it. My *mother* won't tell me."

"Is the profanity necessary?" Baba Yaga asked giving me a pointed look.

"My sister's language is fucking fine," Zach growled, standing up for me again.

Goddess, I *loved* having a brother.

Putting my hand on his arm, I smiled and gave him a squeeze. "It's okay. Baba loves me and I love her. She just hates my foul mouth. It's okay, Zach."

"I think your foul mouth is fucking fantastic," Zach shot back with a quick defiant glance to Baba Yaga.

"Wonderful," Baba Yaga said with an eye roll that beat Zach's earlier winner hands down. "Now there are two of you."

"Yes. Hopefully," I told her. "I need the egg donor to stop lying and tell me the spell she cast."

"I've already heard the story from Mac, Jeeves and Sassy," Baba Yaga said, turning her attention to my mother. "Judith?"

"Yes?"

"A request has been made. I'd suggest you comply with the wishes of the children you didn't deserve to be blessed with. If you don't, things will become quite unpleasant for you."

"I cast no spell," Judith repeated as if on autopilot.

Baba Yaga growled and the room immediately filled with her minions—even Warren and Herb who looked ridiculous. Judith wasn't as bored with the action anymore.

"I *despise* repeating myself," Baba Yaga said as she adjusted her leg warmers and sequined leggings. "What spell did you cast? I'd hate for my boys to have to torture it out of you."

Judith paled considerably and shook her head. "I cast no spell."

Zach was reeling and about to lose it. I wasn't going to let him live with the memory of killing Judith. If it had to be done, I would do it. Zach had lived through enough.

Knocking four minions out of my way, I went to my mother and grabbed her by the hair forcing her to look at me. "You have ruined Zach's life and you tried to destroy mine," I said so viciously she had the decency to blanch. And then I went deadly calm. "Forget about being tortured by the bobble-headed dorks. They've got nothing on me. I will torture you to the edge of death and then I will heal you. I will do this over and over until you tell me what I want to know. The choice is yours… *Mother*."

"I cast no spell," she repeated staring right at me as if she'd never seen me before. "You're asking the wrong question."

WTF? Sassy had seen her cast it… Wait. No, she hadn't. Sassy saw my mother and Henrietta in the room and then Zach and I fell asleep. She felt Zach's chemistry change, but she didn't know why or how. I hated games. I sucked at them, but this was a game of life and death and I was pretty sure I knew the next move.

"Who cast the spell?" I asked, rephrasing my question.

"Henrietta Smith," Judith said.

Tossing her aside like a rag doll so I didn't choke her with my own hands, I jerked my head to Baba Yaga. "She lies. Henrietta Smith is a fucking human. She can't cast a spell that would bind Zach to her for life."

"Not a witch magic spell," my mother said from the heap on the floor where she'd landed. "Voodoo."

Baba Yaga hissed and the room filled with an enchantment so thick, I had to put my hands over my mouth so I didn't choke. Zach powered his way through the magic and found me. Wrapping his arms around me, he held me tight.

"Remember your promise to me, sister," he whispered in my ear.

"I can't kill you," I choked out.

"You promised," he said. "If you truly love me, you will end me."

"What?" Baba Yaga yelled, clapping her hands and dispersing her furious magic. "Who said anything about killing Zach?"

Zach stood tall and pushed me behind him just in case Baba Yaga went for me. He still didn't get it, which made me adore my brother even more. His magic was evident and he was a seriously powerful warlock. Even the minions appeared taken aback. Baba Yaga just stared at him with a strange expression on her face.

"My sister has promised to end me if we couldn't reverse the spell," he said, glaring at Baba and daring her to try and stop us. "If I die, Henrietta dies. There is no other way. If you and your minions could leave the room, I would appreciate it. Leave my mother here. Even if it means nothing to her, she will watch the end result of the game she played with our lives."

My stomach clenched and I felt light-headed. I did love Zach. He was literally a part of me. And even if he couldn't admit it or completely understand it, he loved me too. It had been automatic, the moment we'd laid eyes on each other. It was the natural order of things. Our mother would never understand what she had done because she didn't have it in her to love anyone or anything. But the two beings she gave birth to did know how to love. Maybe that was because Fabio's blood ran through our veins too.

"Would you be willing to meet our father before I grant your wish?" I asked in a strangled voice as tears clogged my eyes and my throat.

"I have no father, Zelda," Zach said flatly. "I will never have a father. I only have you. Please tell Willow that I loved her. I have always loved her and that I'm sorry. And Zorro... please take care of him. He's a beautiful soul."

Nodding, because no words would pass my trembling lips, I hugged the man who I should have known my whole life. It was so fucking unfair that we'd only been given one day together.

"You people are making me cry," Baba Yaga complained, swiping at the mascara running down her face. "No one is going to die today. At least no one in this room."

Zach was having none of it. "You don't seem to understand me," he growled at the surprised and impressed Baba Yaga. "The only way to stop Henrietta Smith is to kill her. The only way to kill her is to end my worthless life. I will not let you stand in my way. I don't give a fuck who you are."

"That was fabulous!" Baba Yaga squealed as Zach and I stood staring at her in complete confusion.

"Umm... dude," I said to my mentor and the woman who I considered my *real* mother. "I think you've lost your shit."

"Not yet," she said with a wink. "Voodoo is magic—very

dark magic. My guess is that this Henrietta is an actual descendant of Marie Laveau."

"She is," Zach said, still ready to have a go at the leader of the witches and warlocks if she tried to stop us.

"Then it can be broken," Baba said with smile. "It can be broken by someone that has dark magic."

"Holy shit," I shouted, scaring everyone. "I have never been so fucking happy to have dark magic in my life. I can do this." And then I froze. "Umm... what do I have to do?"

"What is the opposite of dark?" Baba inquired, seating herself on the back of one of her minions.

"No games," I snapped.

"It's the only way," Baba said. "Play or die."

"You suck," I muttered.

"Yes, I've been told I'm quite good at it," she replied, enjoying herself.

I wasn't even going to tell Zach she was referring to oral skills concerning our father. I'd deal with introducing Zach to Fabio after I figured out how to break the spell.

"Okay. Gross," I snapped. "Can I have a backup player in this game?"

"But of course," she said. "In fact, you will need a second player."

Turning to Zach, I grinned. "Ready to play charades or some kind of shit like it?"

"Born ready," Zach said, taking my hand in his and eyeing Baba Yaga with caution. "We're ready."

"Opposite of dark?" she said.

"Light," Zach answered.

"Correct."

"Opposite of hate?"

"Love," Zach said.

"Opposite of generous?"

"Greedy," Zach said without a second of hesitation.

Baba Yaga nodded. "What has been done to Zach was done in greed, hatred and darkness. Voodoo is quite different than the light magic we practice. However, it can be just as strong, but it's far easier to break its hold."

"Wanna be more specific?" I asked.

"Where would the fun in that be?" she quipped.

I wanted to smack her and I was damn sure Zach wanted to zap her ass, but we both refrained.

"Hold on to me and don't let go," I told Zach and I centered myself and got in touch with both my light and dark powers.

"Come to the wall," Zach insisted, pulling me over to the far side of the room. "I can get inside your head and help you this way."

"Whatever you do, don't fight me," I said, feeling like my stomach had dropped to my toes.

"What are you going to do?" he asked, looking slightly alarmed.

The truth shall set you free or fuck you for all eternity.

"I have no clue. I'm gonna wing it." That was the Goddess's honest truth.

"And this works for you?" Zach asked.

"Eighty-five percent of the time… yes," I replied.

"And the other fifteen percent?" Zach asked, shaking his head.

"Someone ends up with new genitals," I told him with a wince.

"May the Goddess be with us," Zach whispered as he kissed my forehead and took my hands in his. "Go for it, sister."

I just hoped I wouldn't let my brother down… or saddle him with boobs.

CHAPTER SEVENTEEN

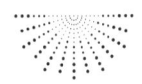

Use it or lose it. That was the motto of the moment.

Zach's hands were warm and strong. We fit together like two pieces of a puzzle. His eyes, identical to mine, were glued to me. His confidence in me was apparent.

With a quick silent prayer to the Goddess for guidance, I let it rip. It was the most important spell I'd ever cast.

Raising my hands high with my brother's still firmly gripped in my own, I closed my eyes.

Goddess on high, please heed my plea,
Darkness is here and I need the key.
Magic so wrong was long ago set to unfold,
Innocence was shattered when the child was sold.
I beg of you please, this fucked up spell you untie,
I refuse to believe my brother will die
I give my blood and my life to reverse the voodoo,
I believe you set me on this course at the convention of...
    umm... doodoo.
In your great wisdom, give us a chance,
And if you do this, our lives you'll enhance.

Oh, and I will try my very best,
To remove the word fucking from any future request.

Zach eyed me for a long moment. I just grinned and shrugged. If my hands were free, I would have flipped him off.

"You wanna add anything?" I asked.

"I do," he replied.

"Be my guest."

The room filled with a shimmering magic I'd never felt before. It was familiar to mine, but without the darkness. Golden sparkles rained down from the ceiling. They tickled my nose and mixed with my own magic that swirled around us. It left me breathless and joyful. It felt so right.

Zach's voice was hesitant. He was clearly rusty. I held my breath and waited.

Goddess above, it's been a long time,
Long ago I gave up and stopped looking for your sign.
If you can forgive me and find it in your heart,
I'd be truly humbled to get a new start.
Deserve it? Well, I might not
But quoting my sister—it's worth a fucking shot.
However, if you choose to refuse me today
Away from Zelda I request you stay.
If this spell doesn't work and things go awry
My twin had promised to help me die.
Love trumps darkness. Love trumps hate.
Please hear our requests and lead us to our true fate.

"So mote it be," Baba Yaga said with a curt nod of approval.

We stood in silence and waited for something to happen. But nothing happened—at all. At the very least, I'd expected an ass-blasting for both Zach and me for the profanity. Zach looked devastated but resigned. I was ready to start over and try again.

And then....

The walls trembled and the floor shook so hard pictures and mirrors fell from the walls and crashed to the floor. The entire building swayed and I was worried we'd be buried under a big pile of decimated pokey—which would suck all kinds of ass. I really wanted to tuck my babies into bed tonight and then play *Princess and the Penis* with Mac. Our bedroom would work just as well as the hotel room.

And then in an instant, the rumbling stopped.

Purple and teal crystal bubbles filled the room making it difficult to see.

I wasn't sure if tricks were being played on my eyes or if I was witnessing something beyond magical. In a glimmering mist, a woman appeared wearing mom jeans, a freakin' t-shirt and chunky dad sneakers. She was the most horribly dressed and yet exquisitely beautiful being I'd ever seen. She was blurry through the bubbles, but she was definitely real. Or maybe a picture had hit me in the head and I was dreaming.

Tears fell from the woman's eyes as she took Zach into her arms and held him close. She smoothed the hair away from his face and placed a kiss on his forehead. I extended my hand and reached out to touch her, but as real as she seemed to me, she was also as transparent as the air.

She smiled and winked and a feeling of true peace washed over me. The Goddess had shown herself. I really wanted to offer to take her shopping, but no words would leave my mouth. Plus, insulting her probably wasn't a good idea. The room was an explosively colorful silent movie. I just hoped the movie would have a happy ending.

Zach writhed in agony and the Goddess held him and comforted him in her strong, loving arms. I watched in awe as a dark mist left his body. The horrible spell floated above him and then disappeared with a sharp crack of lightning as the Goddess waved her hand at the evil that had trapped my brother since the day he was born.

Laying my brother's exhausted body gently on the floor, the Goddess went to Baba Yaga and kissed her forehead. Baba bowed low to the Goddess and her icky minions did the same. I held my breath as the otherworldly vision approached me. Her smile was the stuff that wonderful dreams were made of.

"Thank you," I mouthed, since speech was still impossible.

With a nod and a kiss to my forehead she was gone. The bubbles disappeared and there was no trace that she'd even been here. For a brief moment, I wondered if I'd imagined the entire thing because I so wanted my brother to live and be free.

"She really needs a dresser," Baba Yaga commented as she moved to Zach and helped him to his feet.

"Pot, kettle, black," I muttered under my breath, referring to Carol's own horrendous style as I went to help her with my brother.

"It's gone," Zach whispered hoarsely, getting to his feet.

"Yes, child it is," Baba Yaga said. "You are finally free."

My tears flowed freely as did Zach's and even Baba Yaga's. The icky minions quietly left the room. I made sure to reverse the spell I'd cast on Warren and Herm. I knew it wouldn't make them like me any better, but I didn't like them either.

Plus, I would have felt just awful if I'd forgotten and left them like that. They'd deserved what they'd gotten, but I'd noticed that a few of the other bobble-heads had snapped pictures with their phones. The evidence would be preserved and hopefully keep the little fuckers from messing with me.

"Dude?" I said, grinning through my tears at Zach.

"Yes, dude?" he replied with a grin of his own.

"No more Henrietta Smith."

I could feel his sigh of relief all the way to my toes. It warmed my heart and my... pocket?

"Zelda, you're on fire," Baba Yaga said, pointing to my dress.

"What the fu...?" I shouted as I yanked the flaming stick from my pocket and doused the fire with a wiggle of my nose. How had my wand caught on fire? Had some leftover sparkles gotten in my pocket?

Shitshitshit.

I gasped and felt dizzy. I slapped my hand against the wall so I didn't fall over. I was nauseous and felt a panic seep through my body.

"Willow. Willow is in trouble."

"Fuck," Zach ground out, turned away from us and blasted a hole in the wall that was twice the size of the ones I created in the hotel. "Henrietta found them."

"But she's dead," I said, not following.

"Not yet," Zach said. "She's aging fast and trying to stay alive by any means. I'm out of here."

"I'm with you," I said, grabbing his hand.

And in a blast of identical silver and golden glitter the twins left the building.

We hadn't said goodbye to our egg donor. Hell, I didn't even know if she was still in the room and I didn't care. She was my past—a past I was finally ready to say goodbye to forever. Mac, my babies, my dad, my friends, and now my brother were my future.

However, Willow and Zorro were part of Zach's future and we needed to make sure there was a happily ever after for all the fairy tale characters.

CHAPTER EIGHTEEN

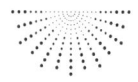

THE TREES IN THE FOREST WHIPPED AROUND LIKE AN F4 TORNADO was blowing through. Branches snapped and the gentle giants wailed in agony. The sound hurt my ears and chilled me to the bone. I could smell the blood and I felt the terror. Where the heck were Willow and Zorro?

Zach glanced around wildly and then took off running faster than any Shifter I'd ever witnessed. My brother defined the term warlock on a new level. There was no way I could keep up with him on my feet, so I flew. As we drew closer to whatever hell we were about to come upon, the air became frigid and the sky grew a menacing black.

Screwing my eyes shut and hoping like hell I didn't run into a tree, I called out in my mind for my cats. I knew they could probably feel my distress. I just hoped the fat fuckers came fast.

"NO," Zach roared as he stopped dead in his tracks and took in the horrifying scene in front of him.

I was only a second behind, but my own scream of shock and fury matched his. Fat Bastard, Jango Fett and Boba Fett arrived in the next instant, covered in paint and hissing like I'd never heard them hiss.

"What da fucks? Dats voodoo magic," Fat Bastard growled as the paint speckled hair on his back stood up.

"What da fucks is happenin' here?" Jango snarled as Boba did some kind of battle hiss and back flipped onto Fat Bastard's kitty shoulders.

"Not sure," I said, scanning the bloody scene. "Just be ready."

"For?" Fat Bastard asked.

"To wing it," I snapped.

"Youse got it, dollface," he said. "Weese will wing da fuck outta dis."

Zorro was gutted from his chest to his groin and bleeding out fast. An enormous blood-spattered hunting knife lay on the ground next to him. Willow lay in a pool of her own blood on the ground beside him. She had clearly already been of *service* to Henrietta. She was as pale as if she was dead, but I could make out her chest barely moving up and down.

Henrietta was right out of her fucking mind. The woman I'd seen at the Witchypoo Convention earlier looked nothing like she had when I'd first laid eyes on her. She was aging by the minute to her true age. Henrietta Smith was screaming like a banshee as she lapped at the blood spurting from Zorro. Her once beautiful form appeared to be about ninety in human years.

"Move away from Zorro and Willow. NOW," Zach roared as blue and green magical sparks punctuated his every word.

"You. What have you done?" the woman screeched in a voice so furiously ugly it made me sick. "You are killing me, you worthless bastard. Come and feed me or I will drain your *friends.*"

"Move away from Willow and Zorro and I will feed you," Zach bargained.

I knew he was lying. He was buying time. It was a matter of only ten minutes or so before she aged to the point of death.

However, a lot of bad things could happen in ten minutes. She continued to suck and lick at the dying Zorro. It was all I could do not to hurl.

"I can blast her," I whispered to Zach. "My aim is good and I can use black magic."

"Is there a chance Zorro or Willow could get hit?" he asked, keeping his eyes on Henrietta.

"Shit," I muttered. "Possibly."

"Then no go," he ground out tersely. "She'll fire spells at me. I'm pretty sure I can deflect them. When I lure her away, get to Zorro and Willow to heal them."

"What do you mean *pretty sure?*" I asked.

"Just do as I say, Zelda. Please," Zach implored, looking wild-eyed with fear for the people he loved—the people he'd never been able to tell he loved and now might never be able to.

"Fine," I agreed as I nodded to my cats. "The wing it part has arrived."

"What's da plan, baby cakes," Fat Bastard asked, hopping up and down and practice- punching the air.

"Can you survive voodoo being thrown at you?" I asked, quickly noticing that the cement diaper was gone. That was good, but I wondered how he'd removed it. My cats were sneaky little buttholes.

"Weese can survive the cauldron of eternal flame in Hell. Of course, weese can survive voodoo," Fat Bastard announced, almost stunning me to silence.

Almost.

"Are you shitting me? The cauldron of eternal flame in Hell is a real thing?" I asked.

"You bet your hot ass it is," Jango Fett informed me with a shudder, making his tubby belly jiggle. "Dat shit is hotter dan two fuckin' hamsters fartin' in a wool sock."

"Youse got that right," Boba said with a thumbs up. "Hotter dan the Devil's asscrack in August."

"Youse guys gots it all wrong," Fat Bastard announced. "I'd say…"

"Nothing," I snapped, trying not to gag at the visuals my idiots had just implanted in my frontal lobe. "You will say nothing. What you will do is deflect any magic thrown at my brother. You feel me?"

"On it," Fat Bastard said, leaping through the air towards Zach as the other two followed suit.

Hopefully, Zach was safe. As gross and appalling as my familiars were, they were insanely good fighters and I adored them. Now we just needed Henrietta to move away from Zorro and Willow.

"Henrietta," Zach called out. "Come to me and you can take my blood. It's much stronger than the blood you're drinking."

She looked up with crazed eyes and called out a spell that sent a jagged spear of explosive voodoo hurtling at Zach. Zach ducked, but thin spear widened as it jettisoned through the air. My scream got caught in my throat as I watched a horror story come to life in front of me.

"If I die, you will die with me," she shrieked sending a second blast on the heels of the first.

"Not today, Satan," Fat Bastard bellowed as his porcine body grew ten times in size in the blink of an eye.

My beautiful fat freak of a cat flew through the air like an enormous furry hairball from hell and took both hits meant for my brother. They ricocheted off the Bastard and flew back at Henrietta. However, she'd already moved. She was fast for a vicious, dying old woman.

With an audible sigh of relief, I thanked the Goddess that the backfire bolt of magic hadn't hit either Willow or Zorro. There was no way they would survive something like that with the shape they were in. I had no clue if they were even still alive, but if they were, I was going to heal the shit out of them. I didn't care if it put me into a coma. I'd survived a coma before. I could survive it again.

The voodoo shots were coming fast and furious. I couldn't believe the old bag still had so much black magic in her at the rate she was aging. Belly crawling so I didn't get struck, I made my way to Willow and Zorro.

Next to me was a huffing and puffing Jango Fett.

"You are supposed to be protecting Zach," I hissed.

"Youse has to be protected too, sweet cheeks," he said with a little kitty grin. "Fat Bastard and Boba gots your boy covered. And I gots your ass covered."

"I love you," I said.

"Can weese get a flat screen TV in the cat room?" he inquired with a sly smile.

"If we all get out of here alive, then yes," I said. "Now help me get to Zorro and Willow."

"Will do, hot potato."

They were in far worse shape than I'd thought. Zorro was all but gone. Willow still had a slim chance. Boba stood guard and took hit after hit as Henrietta was now firing voodoo at anything moving.

"I'm so sorry, Zorro," I whispered as my tears fell into his open chest cavity. "But I'm going to do what I think you would want me to do."

Gently kissing Zorro's forehead goodbye, I turned to Willow.

Her breath came in short shallow spurts and several times I had to stop to avoid the black magic flying willy-nilly through the air. Slowly running my hands over her cold body, I took on the pain that would hopefully make her whole again.

The trees bent forward and watched me work. I wasn't sure if their concern was for Willow or me. Her beautiful green leafy wreath had turned black and the individual leaves were dropping off one by one. I still had no clue what an Adddry was, but it was a beautiful creature.

As if to aid me, the trees above began to drop their leaves. They floated down and surrounded Willow and me and creating a soft bed. Strangely, I no longer felt the wind.

"What da fuck?" I heard Boba grunt as I looked up and gasped.

While the battle raged around us, the trees had moved and made an impenetrable wall protecting us. I could feel the natural energy and I smiled.

"You will keep us safe?" I asked, looking up at the ancient oak and pines.

"*As you wish,*" came the answer on the wind.

"Boba, go and help Zach. I'm shielded here."

"Youse sure, sugar smacks?" he asked, looking up at the trees in awe.

"Positive. Go."

In a little puff of smoke, he was gone.

"Can you help me heal her?" I asked the trees.

"*As you wish.*"

Together we worked on Willow and slowly she came back from near death. These trees were nowhere near as powerful as my minions at home, but they clearly loved Willow and gave everything they had. After a few intense moments, her eyes popped open and she gazed at me in shock.

"Is this the Next Adventure?" Willow asked, trying to get her bearings.

"No, dude," I said with a weary smile. "Not your time yet."

"Zach?" she asked, struggling to sit up.

"Spell's broken. He's buying time until Henrietta dies. My cats have his back. He'll be fine," I told her.

Her smile was positively ethereal and the trees sighed in happiness. I was seriously going to have to look up an Adddry when I got home.

Willow's smile froze on her face. "Zorro?" she demanded in a panic.

I shook my head and tried not to cry. "No."

"Not possible," she insisted, grabbing a low hanging branch and pulling herself to her feet.

Her face went ashen as she spotted her best friend. Moving faster than my eye could follow, she was suddenly right next to him. She began to chant in a melodic language that sounded like a mix of Greek and something I'd never heard. Bright green pops of magic burst around her hands as Zorro's broken body began to very slowly mend.

"Help me," she begged. "I think together we can save him."

"You can heal?" I asked as I crawled over and began to work side by side with her.

She shook her head. "No. I can't, but I have gifts. I can help you."

The trees began to fret and whisper amongst themselves. They were clearly not in favor of Willow using her gifts.

"Hush," Willow said harshly, glaring up at the leaf-covered giants. "I love Zorro like he was my own. Keep your thoughts to yourselves."

The trees weren't happy but obeyed her. I wondered if she understood all trees or just the ones in this forest.

"I'm gonna have to dig deep here," I said as I took a look at what had to be done. My earlier healing of Zorro now seemed like child's play compared to what was about to go down. "If I pass out, it's fine. I'm okay. Just get me home to Mac and he'll know what to do."

"This won't permanently damage you?" she asked, worried.

"Nope. But it's gonna hurt like a motherfucker."

I was correct. The damage done to the goat was so horrendous, I ceased to realize where I was and if anyone was around me. I could feel the light touch of Willow's magic working in tandem with mine, but it grew fainter as I took on

Zorro's more severe internal injuries. Time slowed and my vision blurred. Thankfully, I didn't need to see. I only needed to feel and I could still do that. The sounds of the fight seemed far away or maybe they'd stopped. Minutes felt like years as I used everything I had to mend Zorro back together. Henrietta had to be dead now. Right?

As I felt Zorro's heart start to beat again, I smiled in exhaustion and relief. My insides still burned like they were on fire, but I knew that would stop eventually. With my eyes still closed, I ran my hands over Zorro's body. I froze when a hand grabbed mine.

"Gurlfriend?" Zorro whispered in a ragged voice. "Is that you? Pretty sure my purple leather suit is a goner."

I started to laugh and cry at the same time. Life was good. We were all alive and tonight I would cuddle my twins in my arms and introduce them to their uncle. And of course, I'd finally get to play *Princess and the Penis* with the man I loved more than any other. "Yes it's me. And yes, we need to go shopping for you. The purple leather is toast. I do have some drop crotch pants and chunky dad sneakers you can borrow in the meantime."

"Hell to the no," he choked out with a weak laugh. "Zach? Willow?"

"Both fine," I said as I laid my head on his now closed chest and tried not to fall asleep.

"Willow," Zach cried out in anguish. "Goddess, no."

Just when I thought the shit show was over… it hit the fan.

Again.

CHAPTER NINETEEN

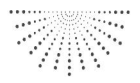

Pulling from energy I didn't know I possessed, my body jerked violently to attention. Zach's magic filled the area and I rubbed my eyes to clear them. Naps were for sissies. I wasn't a sissy. What had gone wrong? Willow was fine.

She wasn't fine now.

Willow lay next to me on the ground. She was not breathing at all that I could see. Her skin was so pale I could see her veins.

"NO," I hissed, mirroring my brother's word. "She was fine. She helped me heal Zorro. This is all fucking wrong."

"Oh my Goddess, no, no, no," Zorro choked out, trying to sit up and get to Willow.

"Stay," I instructed the goat in a harsher tone than I'd intended. "I can't re-heal you *and* Willow."

Had she been hit with voodoo and I didn't realize it? The light touch of her magic had faded as I went in and did the heavy work on Zorro, but I think I would have known if she'd been struck by black magic. She had been right next to me. Granted, I probably couldn't have told you my name during the most excruciating parts of the healing... but how had she been harmed? There wasn't a mark on her body.

The trees swayed and I heard the frantic chattering on the wind. The leafy giants began to weep, sending leaves and twigs flying everywhere.

"Help me, Zelda," Zach ground out desperately as he laid his hands on Willow and sent all the magic he had through her unmoving body. "Wake up, damnit. Willow. Wake up."

Zach looked bad. He was burned and bleeding. My cats were missing a tremendous amount of fur, but they were alive. Voodoo was bad business.

"Henrietta is dead?" I asked as I moved in next to my brother.

"As a fuckin' doornail," Fat Bastard assured me.

"Let me help," I insisted, placing my hands over Zach's and centering myself.

The amount of healing enchantment that entered Willow's body was unheard of. She should be able to run a three thousand mile marathon and come in first with this much magic flowing through her veins.

But Willow didn't move. Her heart rate didn't increase and she grew even paler.

"Tell me what a fucking Adddry is," I hissed, pulling from my core and sending another round of healing magic into the dying Willow.

"She's not an *Adddry*," Zach snapped as he too sent more magic into the woman he loved.

Everything we were doing was in vain. She was fading away. Fast.

She wasn't an Adddry. Willow was not a fucking Adddry. Well, then what was she? Maybe if I knew her species, I could heal her. It was a long shot but... Wait one fucking minute.

"Dry is the second syllable?" I demanded of my brother. The fact that our kind was so cryptic and had so many farked up secret rules was ludicrous.

"No. Not the second," Zach said, taking Willow in his arms and cradling her gently against his broad chest.

Dry… add. Holy Goddess in chunky dad sneakers—wait, the Goddess did wear chunky dad sneakers. Whatever. I was an idiot, but not anymore. Willow was a *dryad*—a freakin' tree sprite. Greek mythology. Bad tree jokes. Walking out of a trunk.

Shit. That was it.

"Give her to me," I shouted and took a limp Willow from my brother's arms.

Flying over to the largest tree I could find, I laid Willow's barely alive body at the base and dropped to my knees. Pulling the wand from my pocket, I pointed it at the tree.

"Take her within you. You are the only thing that can heal her now," I begged.

My wand sparked and sent tendrils of shimmering green mist into the air.

"*It is too late. We warned her,*" the huge oak answered sadly.

"Bullshit," I growled. "I command you take Willow in. I am the fucking boss of the trees. You will do as I wish or I will chop your ass into firewood."

"*If we could, we would,*" the tree whispered. "*She had too much love for others. It is what has finally killed her.*"

"Again, I call bullshit. Love doesn't kill, you wooden jackhole. Hate kills. Apathy kills. Greed kills. Love does *not* fucking kill," I shouted and glanced around wildly. "Any of you—can any of you heal her?"

The trees all drooped forward and I had my answer before they spoke. However, I wasn't about to take no for an answer.

"*If we could, we would. Even together we are not strong enough to mend her,*" another volunteered in a weepy voice.

My head fell to my chest and I felt helpless. I fucking *hated* feeling helpless. I was supposed to be the Baba Yaga In Training even though I still wasn't taking the damned job. But the Baba Fucking Yaga never took no for an answer and I wasn't about to either. I was the Shifter Wanker—the best dressed, most profane damned healer known to witches. If there was any life left in Willow, I was going to save it.

"I'll give you one last chance to obey me," I threatened as I held my twig wand high. "One of you will take her within you. NOW."

"The stick in your hand has more power in it that all the trees in this forest put together," the large oak said softly as his leaves rustled in the wind.

"Seriously?" I asked, glancing up at the stick in my hand. "This twig is more powerful than a forest full of huge trees?"

"It is the simple truth," the tree answered as they all bowed to me and my stick.

Could it be that simple? There was only one way to find out.

"Get up," I commanded to everyone. "NOW. We're leaving."

Zach marched over and tried to take Willow from my arms. "I will not leave Willow here," he growled at me.

"And neither am I, rude dude," I snapped, holding Willow against my body and not letting her go.

I needed to have Willow with me. I knew exactly where I was going. There was a fine chance the rest of the crew could get lost. There was no room for error here. I could still feel the faintest hint of a beat in Willow's heart.

"Where are you taking her?" Zach demanded, trembling with rage and grief.

"Home. I'm taking her home."

"To Assjacket?" Zorro asked, getting to his feet with the help of my cats.

"That's right. Everyone is welcome. I think I can save her there."

Zach was still losing his shit. "And what do you have there that we don't have here?" he demanded.

"My trees, brother. I have my trees."

With a wave of my hand, I left with Willow secured tightly in my arms.

Fat Bastard and the boys knew the way home. Hopefully, Zach would get past his fury and follow. Of course, there was a whole another shit show awaiting him in Assjacket—one named Fabio. But as much as I loved my brother, he wasn't my concern right now.

Willow was.

EPILOGUE

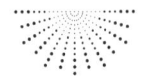

Three weeks later...

"Dear Goddess," Baba Yaga choked out with a wince of horror as we stared out of the bay window in Mac's and my home. Sassy whizzed by on her blue broom screaming with delight. "Please tell me she's not going *commando* while riding on that stick."

I shook my head and groaned. "I really wish I could tell you that, but I'd be lying. Apparently, underpants inhibit the *aerodynamics* on a broom."

"Is that a German word?" Baba Yaga asked with a raised brow and a smirk.

I laughed. "According to Sassy, it's *Canadian*."

"Of course it is," Baba Yaga replied and then turned her attention to the grove of trees in the meadow.

Zach had barely moved from the base of Sponge Bob for three weeks. Fat Bastard, Jango Fett and Boba Fett were my brother's constant shadows. They'd even given up their triweekly poker games to sit with Zach. That was huge for my fat ass familiars. However, Fat Bastard had pointed out that since Zach was basically me with a schlong—the Bastard's words, not mine—Zach was now their responsibility as well. It was pretty clear that the cats drove Zach nuts, but he accepted them.

I wished he would accept a few others, but hopefully time would solve that issue.

My trees had taken Willow in without question and lovingly absorbed her barely alive body into their own massive wooden ones. Sponge Bob was the tree that kept her cradled safely within. Sleepy, Doc, Sneezy and Grumpy had attached their branches to Sponge Bob to provide him with more magic. They were basically now one big assed tree with five trunks—one of the most beautiful things I'd ever seen.

"They look like a child's paper cutout of trees connected like that," Baba Yaga commented idly.

Her statement about the trees was correct. However, her eyes were glued to the man sitting beneath them.

"Does he stay there all the time?" she asked quietly.

I sighed and nodded. "Zach comes inside occasionally. Henry and Audrey are obsessed with him. The feeling is mutual. But most of the time he sits and waits."

"What do the trees say to you?" Baba asked, turning away from the window.

I shrugged and continued to fold toddler clothes. I knew I could use magic, but I was trying to teach my babies that magic didn't solve everything. Folding laundry was good for the soul... or some bullshit line like that.

"My trees don't know Willow's fate. She was so close to death by the time I got her here that her chances of her coming back to us are iffy."

"Does Zach know this?"

"Yep. I told him. He doesn't believe me," I said, pushing the laundry basket away. My soul was fine. "He sends healing power into Sponge Bob every day. Maybe it's helping… maybe it's not. I understand though. He has to do something because the alternative is unacceptable. Losing Mac would make my world meaningless."

"And Fabio?" Baba Yaga asked carefully. "Will your brother talk to him?"

"No."

Zach had flat out refused to even acknowledge our father. I was beginning to get pissed, but my brother was in so much emotional pain, I kept my mouth shut. Now that we'd spent more time together, we were feeling each other's thoughts.

Zach probably knew I was pissed just like I was aware he lived on pins and needles waiting for Willow to come out of the tree. I wondered if Henry and Audrey had the same experience with each other. I was pretty sure they did. If one was unhappy, the other went there too and vice versa.

"You know he's hiding out there," Baba said with a sad smile.

"Who?" I asked, looking back out of the window.

"Fabio. He watches over Zach while Zach watches over Willow."

"Goddess," I said, flopping down on the couch. "Could shit get any more tragic?"

"It could, but it won't," Baba Yaga said with a small smile pulling at her lovely mouth.

"What do you know that I don't?" I demanded.

"You want my job?"

"Fuuuuuck, no," I said with a firm shake of my head and a laugh. "I'm good right where I am. Healing dumbass furballs suits me just fine."

"Then I suppose I can't let you in on the *secret*," she said slyly.

"Wait," I snapped, narrowing my eyes at the badly dressed leader of all witches. "If I say I'll *consider* the Baba Yonightmare job sometime in the far, far, far, far, far, far, *far* distant future, you'll tell me shit?"

"How far?" she inquired casually.

Nothing Baba Yaga did was casual. I was very aware of that.

"Really fucking faaaaaaaaaar," I shot back.

"Then nope. You cannot know that Willow will survive and that someday Zach and Fabio will have a bond that will be so special no one will be able to break it."

My joyous laugh rang out and bounced around the room. Baba Yaga joined me and then pressed her finger to her lips.

"You will tell no one what you have learned," she instructed firmly.

"But Zach is in so much pain," I replied, staring out the window at the depressed male version of myself. "It seems cruel not to tell him Willow will be fine eventually."

"That's the rule about seeing the future," Baba Yaga stated.

"Rules suck," I told her.

"This is true, sometimes," she acknowledged with a tilt of her head and a sigh. "However, the natural order of things must take place, Zelda. It's what the Goddess intended. What Zach is feeling right now is not just panic about Willow. He's led a life that none of us can imagine. Now that he's free, he's working his way through the darkness that had imprisoned him. Hopefully, he's also letting it go. He's not ready for his happily ever after yet and the Goddess is well aware of it."

"Dude, you are so freakin' smart. Even if I wanted your job, I would suck huge assmonkeys at it," I said staring at her.

"You think I haven't screwed up?" Baba demanded as she began to spark. "Do you honestly think the fact that your brother—your *twin,* no less and one of the people I was *supposed to keep safe*—was trapped into blood slavery doesn't keep me up at night?"

I was silent after that admission. I felt exactly the same way. The enormity of what Carol was in charge of was the real reason I couldn't and wouldn't take the job. I was barely responsible enough to use my magic correctly. I didn't want to imagine a time where I was in charge of everyone else's.

"Pretending to be you… or the one in charge was kinda sucky," I admitted.

"But you didn't back down from anything that was thrown at you," Baba Yaga pointed out. "You switched witches beautifully—just like I knew you would."

She was right and wrong. My performance was not what I would describe as beautiful, but I didn't back down. Honestly though, I didn't want to relive what happened three weeks ago any time soon. But yes, I'd done it. I was proud of all I had done. And if presented with something similar? Yep—I would tackle it again.

Shitshitshit.

"Let my kids grow up first," I blurted out before I knew what was going to fly from my lips.

Baba's grin was wide and she nodded her head with satisfaction.

I signed dramatically and zapped my own ass on purpose. I was all kinds of an idiot. But before I could take any of it back, Baba Yaga poofed away in a cloud of peach glitter.

"Great, the freak show will hold me to that," I muttered.

"How do I look?" Zorro inquired as he bounced into the great room grinning from ear to ear.

"Umm..," I wasn't sure how to answer without insulting him.

He and Zach both had rooms in our home until they didn't want or need them. I was perfectly okay if they wanted to live with us until the end of time. While Henry and Audrey were obsessed with Zach, they adored the ground Zorro walked on. He shifted to his goat constantly and gave them rides through the meadow. Audrey had conjured up goat horns for both her brother and herself and they wore them all the time. I finally had to put an end to that when they gored the living crap out of Bermangoggleshitz's backside. Roy didn't give two hoots, but it was a very bad habit to shove your horns into the asses of your guests. I was not raising heathens. Not to mention, I wasn't too fond of healing Roy's butt.

"Gurlfriend," Zorro sang as he twirled around the room. "Am I not fabu?"

How to answer that inquiry without devastating my new friend…

The goat was wearing the tightest black pants and shirt I'd ever seen. I had no clue how he'd even gotten them on. They were so dang tight, his *religion* was showing. Of course, when you added a long black cape, a black eye mask, and a squat sombrero looking hat with red pompoms hanging from it, you had a seriously hot mess.

"Are you going somewhere special in that… umm… getup?"

"To rehearsal!" he squealed. "I'm starring in the Assjacket Community Theatre's new musical production of *Zorro, the Gay Blade*!"

Biting down on my lips so I didn't scream in horror, I just thanked the Goddess that I hadn't been blackmailed into performing again. The musical version of *Mommie Dearest* had been enough for my entire lifetime.

"Wow," I said—because *"Holy shit—are you fucking joking?"* wasn't nice.

"Fabio is directing and Sassy is playing all the women's roles in the show. It will be very avant-garde. I. Love. Assjacket," Zorro squealed as he pranced out of the room.

And Assjacket loved Zorro. Every single Shifter, witch and warlock thought that goat hung the moon. He was even thinking about running for Mayor since we didn't have one… or need one, actually.

The five Shifters that Mac had relocated from Lexington to

Assjacket had indeed been greeted by Bob the *unibrow* beaver. However, that turned out to be no big deal since three of the incoming new members of our community had unibrows of their own.

We'd officially added three beaver Shifters and two llama Shifters to our fold. I just hoped they weren't as clumsy as the rest of the dorks who lived here.

Sadly, Lexington was now pretty much magic free. Of course, they still had Verruca Trotcackler…

"Mommy," Henry squealed as he flew into the room followed by a giggling Audrey. "Me and Awey wanna go love on Uncle Zach."

"Yessssss, Mommy!" Audrey announced as she showed me the three peanut butter and jelly sandwiches she'd made. My little girl had not used magic. The sandwiches verged on gross with jelly squishing out of the sides and a big glob of peanut butter sitting on top of the bread. They were perfect. "We make lunch for Zachy! He be hungry now."

"I bet he is," I said, showering my precious babies with kisses. I was now wearing peanut butter and jelly all over my face and shirt, but it was a look I loved. "I think it's a great idea."

"Yayayayayayay!" they shouted as they flew out of the open window and down to the meadow.

Zach's face lit with happiness as they landed on top of him, smearing him with his lunch. Being with his niece and nephew were the only times I'd seen him truly smile since he'd arrived.

I'd spent plenty of time sitting under Sponge Bob with my brother, but our talks were more serious and emotional. We had a hell of a lot of catching up to do. The one person we never spoke of was our egg donor. We hadn't made the rule with words—we somehow just knew. Eventually, we would have to discuss her but not any time soon.

Audrey was busy doing a wild little dance for Zach. Her

adorable red curls bounced as she twirled like a toy top on speed.

Henry—not to be outdone by his sister—was busy turning acorns into toads. Whatever. If we ended up with an infestation, I'd turn them into something else that worked well around trees.

I still wondered if bagworm Shifters were a real thing but I decided not to ask.

I smiled as I watched them eat. My new normal was turning out to be better than anything I could have imagined for my life.

"I have a great idea," Mac said coming up behind me and wrapping his strong arms around me.

"Do you?" I asked as I reached around and grabbed his jeans clad perfect ass. "I have some ideas too."

Mac spun me around so my body was pressed flush with his. My girly parts perked up and I could feel that his *part* was quite happy to see me too.

"I reserved a hotel room for us," he said, brushing his lips against mine and making them tingle. "We never did get to play *Princess and the Penis*."

I was caught between a rock and a hard place... no pun intended. As much as I *really* wanted to play *Princess and the Penis*, I didn't want to leave my babies.

"Umm..." I began, staring straight at his chest because eye contact would give me away. "That sounds... you know... umm..."

"Terrible?" he asked hopefully.

My eyes jerked to his. Did Mac not want to play *Princess and the Penis* with me?

"Explain yourself," I said, trying to slip out of his arms so I could properly pout and blow something up.

Mac was having none of it. His arms trapped me like steel bands.

"Fine," Mac said sheepishly. "I didn't want to sound like a boring dad, but the hotel was for you—not me. I felt bad that we missed out on hotel sex since you were so excited about it. I don't want to go away from Henry and Audrey."

"Wait. So you *do* still want to play *Princess and the Penis?*" I asked, making sure I was following.

Grabbing my hand and placing it on his *penis*, he grinned. "I definitely want to play *Princess and the Penis*... and my Bon Jovi does too."

"Goddess, what a relief," I said, wrapping my arms and legs around him. "I thought you didn't want to have sex with me."

"Zelda, I spend ninety-nine percent of my day thinking about having sex with you," he said with a panty melting grin.

"That is so hot," I squealed and I rubbed my excited body against his. "What do you do with the other one percent of your time?"

"Everything else I have to do in life," he said with a laugh as he began walking us toward our bedroom. "How much time do you think we have?"

"They just went down to eat lunch with Zach. I'd say an hour," I told him, nipping at his neck.

"And Zorro?"

"He's at a rehearsal for Assjacket Community Theater's upcoming musical version of *Zorro, the Gay Blade*," I told him, trying not to giggle. I failed.

"Not touching that one, Princess," he said with a chuckle as he tossed me on the bed and jumped on beside me. "You ready to play, baby?"

"I was born ready," I said, pulling him on top of me.

"That what I like to hear."

I knew it would take time for Zach to be okay, but I knew in my heart he would. Hopefully, Willow would join us in the near future and they could work out their own shit together.

Fabio was kind of breaking my heart. His desire to know his

son was so plain to see. He wore his heart on his sleeve and his sorrow on his face. But I knew the *secret* now, and in time, that would resolve itself too.

Right now, it was time for me—me and the hottest werewolf in Universe.

I was the best damned princess Mac had ever seen.

And his penis?

Let's just say it rocked my world.

The Princess and the Penis was definitely a keeper.

—The End…for now—

NOTE FROM THE AUTHOR

If you enjoyed *Switching Witches*, please consider leaving a positive review or rating on the site where you purchased it.

Reader reviews help my books continue to be valued by resellers and help new readers make decisions about reading them.

You are the reason I write these stories and I sincerely appreciate each of you!

Many thanks for your support,
~ Robyn Peterman
www.robynpeterman.com

EXCERPT: BAD PANTHER

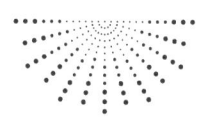

ALIEN GUARDIANS OF EARTH, BOOK 1

DONNA MCDONALD

CHAPTER ONE

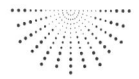

Somewhere in the wilds of North Dakota...

Dr. Sugar Lee Jennings was so far into the wilderness that even her GPS wasn't registering her location. When she'd bought her expensive hiking watch, she'd paid extra for that feature and it was supposed to work everywhere. Well, screw that—and obviously her too—because in the end finding the cave had been nothing but sheer luck and trusting her intuition.

Now that she was actually facing the cave's not-breached-in-centuries entrance, Sugar decided it was a toss-up as to whether she found the place creepy or heard it beckoning her to come discover its secrets. The weirdness of such thoughts was enough to have her lecturing herself aloud.

"Sugar Lee, get a grip. You really didn't have to come all the way out here in nowhere land to prove your dead daddy was right about your lack of common sense."

Pulling up her mental panties, she walked into the cave and vowed to toss out all her *Indiana Jones* movies when this hair-brained adventure was over. Such movies had made her boring childhood more tolerable, and inspired her current career, but they'd also made her think hiking into the wilderness of North Dakota alone wasn't a completely insane thing to do to prove a damn theory.

"This is not insane," Sugar said to the dank walls. "This is my journey to fame and fortune. I am here to find it."

Sugar didn't know why no one before her had bothered to track down the Third Cave Of The Beringians. If she was right about the cave having been trapped in a glacier for ages—and Sugar was reasonably sure she was—her footsteps were the first to disturb the ancient dust on the cave floor in tens of thousands of years. Excitement over that fact didn't make the cave any less creepy though, but it did give Sugar the motivation needed to press on.

She'd drawn the map to the cave herself from clues she'd found in about a hundred different books. One of Athena the Ancient's blades was hidden here—she just knew it was. Her instincts were singing.

Not that she had managed to unearth any conclusive evidence. Tales of Athena's existence read like Homer's stories of the mythical Ulysses. Athena was a legendary metal-smith from Earth's ancient pre-history who had allegedly merged organic matter with metallic substances to bestow some sort of sentience in the weapon.

Why had a technological genius focused on such a thing?

Honestly, Sugar had no idea. Only a computer geek living in his mother's basement would find the whole "sentient blade" thing as fascinating as she did. There was no way to explain Athena the Ancient without the story sounding like science fiction instead of actual history.

Maybe she was crazy for coming alone, but she practically could hear the Smithsonian-worthy artifact calling to her inside her head. *"Sugar,"* it whispered. *"Come find me."* She'd definitely come too far to back out.

Yes, she knew hearing the artifact speaking in her head was utter nonsense. Maybe her energy was dipping low after her four-mile-hike to get to the cave. Sugar stopped walking and wondered if she should eat the protein bar in her coat pocket before continuing.

She tucked her flashlight under her arm to free her hands which ended up tilting the beam down to the dirt floor. Her action made the top of cave darker… and that's when she saw it. Up ahead, a soft light glowed in the cave's stark blackness.

Was she having a hallucination?

There was always the possibility that she was sniffing some underground chemical seeping into the cave. Maybe she was getting high on chemical fumes… or ancient carbon dioxide.

A few more steps forward took her far enough into the interior to totally lose the light from the cave opening behind her. Squinting at something ahead in the dark, Sugar fought the sudden apprehension she felt and bravely turned off her flashlight.

Her heartbeat picked up speed when the cave ceiling glowed golden.

What else could be glowing in the cave? It had to be the artifact.

Flipping on her flashlight again, Sugar inched forward following the beam now.

"Sugar."

The artifact whispered her name… *and then did it a second time.*

Cold chills covered her arms even through all the layers of clothing she'd worn for her hike.

Standing next to her discovery now, Sugar could see the outline of a box. The cover was definitely emitting light of some sort.

She turned her flashlight off again and bent to carefully set it on the cave floor. She also slipped her heavy hiking pack off and did the same with it.

"*Sugar.*"

This time her name vibrated in the air. Her imagination had suddenly developed a deep voice and had obviously gone native on her.

Absolutely nothing Sugar had studied for either of her degrees had covered any of this. A talking artifact who recognized her was way too strange for her to take seriously.

It had to be the result of bad air in the cave.

Next time she went artifact hunting, she was bringing an oxygen tank and a breathing mask.

"Ignore the voices. Keep to the plan," Sugar ordered herself.

Channeling *Indiana Jones* and his fictional bravery once more, she inspected the resting place of the glowing box. For a brief moment, she wished she was back in the cheap motel she'd rented yesterday. Unfortunately, the motel was a four-hour hike out the forest and then an additional sixty-mile drive away from the location of the cave.

Leaving when she'd come so far didn't make sense and her logical mind insisted that being afraid was totally ridiculous. After all, couldn't she just retrieve her flashlight and hiking pack and leave if her concerns grew too large?

Who would know about her cowardice but her?

The answer to her internal debate ended up being a resounding 'no' to leaving for any reason because something in her stubborn, too-curious DNA wouldn't let her.

This was the best chance she'd ever have to prove her theories. It might be her only chance.

And God, she loved being right.

Wouldn't she enjoy all her peers knowing she'd found something to prove Earth's pre-history was more advanced than most believe?

Sugar ran her fingers lightly over the glowing box and

wiped away several inches of dust and dirt. Two glowing white handprints were on the lid. They were both outlined in tiny blue tubes filled with what appeared to be a circulating liquid of some sort.

"Are you someone's practical joke or an honest-to-god ancient artifact?" Sugar asked the box. Her surprise at its modern appearance was precisely why ancient people ended up believing in gods.

Wanting the full experience of whatever secrets the box held for her, Sugar pressed her sweaty palms into the handprints. A warm heat stroked across them and made her chuckle. "Gee, that feels nice… and a bit strange. What in the world are you?"

"*Genetics validated. Host accepted.*"

The cryptic statement echoed loudly inside her brain… and also made her laugh. It was like she was starring in her own science fiction movie.

A grin spread across her lips. "*Accepted?* You accept me? That's awfully polite of you."

Sugar giggled about responding back as her hands slid off the handprints and ran possessively over the entire golden surface of her find.

"Well, I accept you too, pretty gold box, because you are going to make me a very rich and famous woman. But just to be clear here, we both know the whole talking-to-me thing is just a carbon dioxide hallucination I'm having."

As she stared at it, the lid retracted—or disappeared altogether—Sugar couldn't be sure which.

Before she could investigate the mechanism supporting such a surprising action, she glanced inside and noticed a long golden dagger glowing up at her from the bottom of the box.

Her fisted hands went into the air as Sugar excitedly hopped around in the dark.

"*Yes! Yes! Yes! I knew it!* There really is a blade. It has to be one of Athena the Ancient's blades. Give the woman her million dollar finder's fee, people. Move over, Indiana Jones, Dr. Sugar Lee Jennings is a freaking archaeological genius."

Once she was in control of herself once more, Sugar was vastly relieved when the box didn't respond to her happy dance over her discovery. The silence in her head hopefully meant her brains cells weren't dying from poisoned air at a galactic rate after all.

Elation to see an actual blade resting in the box pushed her earlier fears aside. Sugar grinned as she lifted the golden blade from its home. Rather than looking like an actual weapon, the glowing golden dagger instead resembled a ritual athame. There were no edges on the blade sharp enough for cutting. But there was a strange vibration against her hand as the lights on it pulsed in the darkness.

Sugar brought the artifact closer to inspect it. In the light of its soft glow, she could see strange markings covered nearly every inch of the gleaming metal surface.

Was it truly gold? It certainly looked like it. But what if it was a new type of metal—an ancient alloy of some sort?

Rather than take time to retrieve her flashlight from the floor to get a better look, Sugar decided to return the blade to the box and head outside with her treasure.

"Lord, I can't wait to carbon date you," she told the gleaming object in her hand.

Still gripping the blade's handle, she ran a free finger over what seemed to be a symbolic language etched in the surface. Her action must have triggered something because the light being emitted from the marks suddenly changed from a soft glowing gold to a pulsating, iridescent green.

What had to be a million tiny lights began to dance under the top layer of what looked like transparent gold to Sugar's eyes. The artifact was an absolutely fascinating form of ancient metallurgy. This discovery would definitely count as an archaeological, career-making find.

"Physical evaluation completed. No impediments detected. Merge protocol activated."

Great, Sugar thought, looking around her in the dark. She was back to hearing the talking in her head. Oxygen—she obviously needed oxygen.

When her palms started to sweat again, Sugar laughed at the strange statements.

Merge protocol? Where the hell had that craziness come from?

She'd just made the freaking archaeological find of a lifetime. She refused to be afraid of her own hallucinations.

Narrowing her eyes, she glared at the blade. "Listen here, artifact. Nobody merges with Sugar Jennings unless she damn well wants them to."

As the significance of her words hit her, Sugar rolled her eyes in the dark.

"Oh, for goodness sake, I can't even believe I'm actually talking to a... *a thing*. That's definitely enough carbon monoxide sniffing for me. I have got to get out of here while I still have some brain cells left. Back you go into your pretty little box."

Sugar was trying unsuccessfully to return the blade to its former resting place when strange utterances began rapidly coming from the blade itself.

She brought it close again. What the hell? Did it have a speaker in it? Was this thing some clever geek's idea of a joke?

But wait... the voice in her head had been communicating in English. She sure wasn't hearing English now.

She lifted the blade to her ear and listened as closely as she could. The artifact was definitely making sounds that seemed like language of some sort.

The words sounded like... *what?* Sugar couldn't decide.

The utterances were rhythmic, spaced equally apart, and...

"Holy shit. Are you doing some sort of a countdown?"

Sugar warily held the blade at arm's length as survival panic hit her full force. Her instincts took over and excitement over her find fled. For all she knew, what she'd found could be some sort of homemade bomb.

She needed to get out of the cave. She needed to do it now.

Sugar tried once more to return the blade to the golden box—only the freaking thing no longer fit. Was the box shrinking? How could that be possible?

She was still pondering things when the blade suddenly ceased its uttering and switched to emitting a loud, steady hum that seemed to be increasing in resonance.

"Okay. I'm fucking done with this shit. Money and fame are not worth getting blown up," Sugar yelled as she glared at the blade.

Before she could put the artifact down on the stones and make her escape, the damn thing exploded in her hand and sent out blinding white light in all directions. The impact of the explosion knocked her to her knees.

Sugar glanced around the dark cave but couldn't see where the blade had gone. Her palm where it had been was on fire. She suspected a burn but there was no light now to check.

Then an excruciating pain in her chest made itself known and shut out all other thoughts and concerns.

"Merge initiated. Symbiosis now in progress."

Unclear about what she heard, Sugar wanted to ask the voice in her head to repeat what it had said. Only a pain-filled gasp actually escaped her burning throat when she tried to talk.

She must have fallen after the explosion. Her entire body felt like she'd been punctured with hundreds of flaming needles. Everything hurt.

The darkness of the cave soon descended on Sugar's mind, but as she went under she could have sworn she heard the blade speaking more of its strange language.

CHAPTER TWO

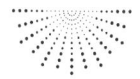

S*ix hours later...*

W*ith her head throbbing from some sort of fall that had* left her lying on the dirty cave floor in total darkness, Sugar fought to push her still aching body upright but didn't get far. She groaned loudly with the struggle. Her hand swept out across the floor and luckily found the flashlight she'd brought with her.

Sugar flicked it on and spun the light around to see where she was. She found she was lying at the bottom of a large pile of carefully stacked stones.

Why in the hell hadn't her freaking flashlight been on the whole time? Without it, she must have run into the stone cairn in the dark and knocked herself the hell out.

Sugar pushed the rest of the way to her knees and felt her aching body wobble with the effort. Her head felt like it was going to roll off her shoulders.

Then... *wow*... she put a hand to her forehead as she suddenly recalled a dream she'd had about finding the artifact.

There had been a glowing box with handprints. There had been a golden blade that talked to her in a language she hadn't understood.

Feeling like a true idiot now for letting her imagination run wild, Sugar groaned in mortification as she knelt on the cold cave floor.

She really, really needed to get some fresh air into her lungs. There had to be carbon monoxide in the cave.

Poisoned air was the only way to explain her having such a vivid, colorful dream like that, especially when she'd obviously knocked herself out on the pile of rocks beside her.

Her disappointment over not finding any ancient artifact was keen, but the flashlight sweeping the cave walls confirmed her search was done. The cave ended abruptly just behind the tower of stacked stones.

Damn it all to hell.

There'd be no Indiana Jones glory for her today.

Sugar checked her watch to see how long she'd been unconscious, but it didn't seem to be working correctly. The last time it showed was six hours ago. So much for buying a top of the line model. The watch must have broken from shock when she fell.

As Sugar stood on wobbly legs, she inspected the cairn and saw a clean spot on top. Had she touched it before she fell? She reached out her fingers to feel the smooth area. Her brain reached for a memory, but none came.

"Get some damn oxygen, Sugar," she told herself sternly.

Head hurting, Sugar retrieved her hiking pack, pulled it onto her sore shoulders, and started the dirty trek back out of the cave. She walked head down while fighting hard not to feel super sorry for herself.

Coming into the cave, she'd been so sure that she was going to find something valuable—something that would make her career. Now? Well, now she'd be starting all over again. Failure hurt, but she'd survived that before.

At the cave entrance, Sugar stopped completely. Breathing fresh air, at last, was fantastic, but the sunlight did nothing to ease her pounding head.

Blinking several times to adjust to the brightness, Sugar suddenly felt her entire chest vibrating like it had turned into a giant cell phone.

There was pain too—pain she couldn't identify. It went deep and radiated to all her bones.

Maybe she'd hit those rocks harder than she thought when she fell. She looked down at her clothes and was shocked to see her shirt was shredded in the front.

"Damn it, Sugar. What in the double-L hell happened to you in there?"

She spat the question as she searched her destroyed shirt for the source of the damage. Then she noticed a golden spear end pointing up to one shoulder. Touching it hurt, but the smooth vibrating metal beneath her exploring fingers told her it wasn't any sort of tattoo.

She looked on the other side of her chest and found another metal spear-like point matching the first.

Peering down between her breasts, she saw there was one in the middle of her sternum as well, but it stopped midway between her generous cleavage that blocked the view of the rest of it.

It looked a bit like she'd fallen on Poseidon's trident and accidentally pushed it into her chest. She couldn't see it without a mirror but she felt some sort of metal band wrapped around her rib cage from front-to-back... and well... it was vibrating too.

Wanting to stop the pain any way she could, Sugar pulled her nearly destroyed shirt together and clenched it closed with her fist. Once all the trident was covered, the vibration immediately stopped, as did the incredible pain in her head. Whatever it was it didn't like the light.

"What the ever-loving fuck happened in there?" Sugar demanded as a fresh panic of biblical proportions swept over her. She turned and glared behind her.

Holding her mangled shirt closed with one hand, Sugar ran all the way back to her rented vehicle, her anxiety growing with every footfall on the ground. It was only when she was driving back to her motel that she realized she'd just run the four-hour hike to the car in a little over thirty minutes without ever once getting tired or winded.

"I'm officially changing careers. Screw having freaking adventures," Sugar declared. A golden vibrating metal parasite was now taking up residence in her chest.

The science fiction stories she'd loved all her life had never come close to shit like this in reality. However, memories of every horror movie she'd ever watched were now playing non-stop in her mind.

She couldn't recall anything about what had happened in the cave before she got knocked out, but for damn sure, she'd found something while in there.

Or something had found her.

Now what was it intending to do with her?

CHAPTER THREE

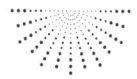

In Axel of Rodu's Catskill Mountain lair...

Like most felines he'd come across on the planet, Axel liked being where he wanted to be and only when he wanted to be there. After trying many places to live in his six hundred years of life, this private sanctuary hidden deep in a forest was the only location where he'd ever felt truly at peace with himself.

His current residence wasn't his favorite jungle vacation spot or the desert lands his feline mother favored. The mountain base hideout he called home in the Catskill Mountains of New York was evergreen and blessedly free of most creatures he didn't want to see.

"Max, fetch," Axel demanded in a loud voice, throwing a limb he'd broken off of a nearby fallen tree.

When the wolf didn't run as instructed, Axel looked down at the creature who huffed indignantly at his feet.

"We had a deal, Maxwell," Axel said, pointing at where the stick had landed. "Do you want me to send you back to your pack and let them carry out your punishment? You know that staying here means you agree to be my pet for the duration."

The unhappy wolf whined, hung his head, and stared at the ground. When his head lifted, the creature sent back a reply.

You may consider yourself a cat, Axel, but I do not consider myself a dog.

"The full moon arrives Thursday, Max. Fetch the stick for me like a good wolf, and perhaps I will allow you to shift to human then—for a few hours at least."

The wolf's head came up swiftly. Max took off running to where the stick had landed. Axel snorted as his reluctant detainee sent him a disgusted look before snatching up the piece of wood in his mouth.

Max started back toward him, glaring his wolf eyes, then suddenly dropped the stick and ran off with a whimper.

"Maxwell! We weren't finished. Get back here with that stick," Axel shouted.

"Axel, stop yelling at that poor creature you're tormenting. Is that any way for a Lyran prince to act?"

Axel swung and stared at the ascended Lyran feline standing behind him. Great. How long had she been watching?

"Queen Nyomi," he said, dropping to one knee and bowing his head. He knew he was in more trouble when she sighed loudly.

"Thirty hours of childbirth to bring you into this life and all I get from my son is normal deference? I get that from everyone. Stand up and hug me, Axel. Prove I chose your Earthling father well."

Axel rose and started toward her only to be stopped by a raised hand and twitching ears. "Not in your purely human form while we're talking business. I can only handle your father in that condition."

"Right," Axel said automatically, shifting his human skin until his face more closely resembled hers. Now they both looked like they belonged to the feline branch of the Lyran race they were descended from. At his mother's approving nod, Axel moved forward and embraced the female who'd given birth to him. "I am glad to see you, Mother. It's been nearly a year since you visited me."

"Yes, it's been too long," Nyomi agreed solemnly, hugging her eldest child of Rodu tightly before pushing him away. "I've been swamped with royal duties while you've been amusing yourself here in your lair. I wish this was a purely social visit, but I came today because I have another little matter I need you to take care of for me."

"Another little matter?" Axel repeated the request with a snort, releasing her arms to laugh. "Your little matters are never little, Mother. I almost got decapitated solving your little matter last time."

"I admit I underestimated Lord Garmin's viciousness, but I could not allow my favorite human to be killed while regenerating. Your father helped me bring a true Lyran prince into this often barbaric, ungrateful world. Of all the humans walking his planet, your father deserves as many lives as my people can give him."

Axel inclined his head once. "I honor the human male who helped create me which is precisely why I ended Lord Garmin's life."

Nyomi purred in pleasure. "Yes, my son is the most feared creature on both our planets…" She stopped and made a face. "Or at least you were until recently."

Axel lifted a brow. "That's an extraordinarily strange comment even for you, my queen. You made sure no one was trained better than me. Who is deadlier?"

Nyomi looked off, her small ears twitching again. "No one intentionally but I think someone has found one of Athena the Ancient's sentient blades."

"Sentient blades?" Axel repeated in surprise. "Most believe

they are a myth, especially the sentient part. You're talking about advanced artificial intelligence. My sister's advances in that area exceed any Earth human's or Lyran's. Not even Gina of Rodu has found a way to make that work."

Nyomi shook her regal head. "The sentient blades are not a myth, Axel. I don't know how well your teachers covered those artifacts in your Ancient Earth History classes, but the blades are weapons from a time on Earth before the feline Lyran Guardians came here to live. Lyran records show evidence of some very sophisticated weaponry being developed long before Earth's current history began being recorded."

Axel nodded that he heard. "As I recall, Athena's blades were developed for warriors. Why would one of them want to join with a mere archaeologist?"

Nyomi's mouth lifted on one corner. "It's true that Lyran records say the blades were only sentient after they were joined with the highest and noblest of warriors. However, Earth legends of the blades are not so clear on the matter. Maybe Athena's creation was desperate to be joined to a host after twenty thousand years of dormancy."

Axel rubbed his chin. "Do you wish me to subdue the blade and send it back into hibernation?"

Nyomi stared at her son and fought not to be impatient with the child who was supposed to be grooming himself to replace her. "Would you willingly return to a lifeless existence of never having been born?"

Since he had no wish to offend his mother... or his queen, Axel shook his head. "No, I suppose not," he said.

Nyomi walked a short distance and glanced out into the trees. "I'm guessing neither will the blade now that it's awake again. It's a very powerful artifact—I fear much more powerful than even you. This situation must be handled very carefully. Current Earth may be primitive, but there is much about its technological past that we do not yet know."

Axel nodded once in acknowledgment though he had trouble imagining anything or anyone alive on the planet being more powerful than he was. He told himself it wasn't arrogance to feel that way. He just hadn't seen any evidence that pointed away from his conclusion about his worth as a warrior.

"What would you like me to do about it then?" Axel finally asked.

Because the matter was so serious, Nyomi turned to look in her son's eyes as she answered. "The archaeologist who found the blade is still finding out what comes with living with such power. Every greedy group on the planet is hunting the blade's new host—both human and paranormal factions. The blade must remain where it is until its champion has either bonded with it completely or died trying to."

Axel winced internally. Death from finding an ancient artifact? That would certainly be a tough break for a nosy archaeologist, he decided as he listened to his queen.

"I'm guessing you want me to be the human's bodyguard until the human and the blade part company."

Nyomi laughed. "So you do understand—thank the ancestors. Yes, Axel, I want you to guard the blade. More than that though, I was hoping you would attempt to train its human host to be a warrior. The initial joining is done. All we can do now is try to make the human at least a little worthy of the entity she carries."

"*She?*" Axel repeated it as a question, his mouth forming an ironic smile. "In my studies, they said the sentient blades were created for males."

"No—they said they were created for warriors."

"Which were primarily male," Axel insisted.

"Your studies were based on general information about a very advanced Earth culture that disappeared thousands of years ago. What few records we've found are not enough to assume any one thing is right one hundred percent of the time, especially about gender roles."

"Agreed," Axel said with a reluctant shrug. "So who do you think Athena the Ancient was then? Was she a warrior?"

"From my studies, I have come to believe that Athena was not from Earth at all. Whatever her planetary origin, it's likely that she was considered some sort of warrior by the Earth people of her time. But even if she was just an extremely advanced human, there are always exceptions. You are an exception among Lyrans."

"But a woman warrior that powerful..." Axel began and then stopped to shake his head.

He had several sisters who were brilliant and fierce, but he didn't think of them as warriors like himself. In fact—what did he think about women fighting? Undoubtedly, nothing his queen would approve of.

Sighing in frustration, Nyomi's disappointed gaze slid over her mega-intelligent, but clueless son. "I see skepticism in your eyes and it makes me very angry at you. The Lyrans—*our* people, Axel—chose *me* to be Earth's primary guardian, not any Lyran male. They chose me because I was an intelligent, fair-minded warrior who was willing to do whatever it took to see the humans of Earth progress in a way that fosters planetary peace in our shared galaxy."

Axel lowered his gaze. "Forgive me, my queen. I meant no disrespect to you or your talents."

Nyomi huffed. "I always do forgive you, but perhaps that is your problem. I should have insisted you mate Rian centuries ago. Living with a full Lyran female mate might have corrected that gender-biased selfishness you've developed from consorting with those weak-minded human females you favor."

"Despite the genetics of my human father, my sexuality is Lyran. I prefer brief partners who serve a practical purpose when sharing my bed. I do not think my DNA includes the ability to love any female—Earthling or Lyran—the way a human male like my father is obviously capable of doing."

Queen Nyomi snarled in disbelief. "Really? What about the human female who runs that agency you align with? You felt something more than lust for her."

Axel grunted and turned away. "It fluttered through my chest briefly and passed before I even recognized it was a genuine attraction. I do think it was a pity that she chose those two stone idiots as mates. What a waste of womanhood."

"Gargoyles aren't real stone," she reminded him. "Remember that each gargoyle's soul remains human regardless of the change to the original container. The ancient magic that created their bodies is to be respected just as much as the incredible power that forged the sentient blade you're getting ready to encounter. Disrespect of such power is for ignorant humans. It is not something a Lyran Earth Guardian can indulge in, not even in jest."

"I concede to your greater wisdom about ancient Earth magic, but I know my mind quite well when it comes to my sexual needs. I have no urge to mate permanently with any female and I find no fault with the way I have chosen to meet them," Axel said, bowing his head.

"Oh, my dear boy, your sexual selfishness is nothing but male self-delusion. One day you will learn that truth. I hope it happens soon."

"And I hope that it never happens at all," Axel said calmly.

Tired of her and Axel's debate, Nyomi pulled her mind back to the real reason she came to see her son. "We could argue your eventual epiphany for hours, but unfortunately, we have more important things to discuss today. That agency you pretend to work for is going to be calling you soon."

"Are you for certain?"

Nyomi glared at her son. "Yes. The archaeologist who found

the blade has gone to them for help. Take the assignment and bring the blade's host here to your lair. But do not seek to sexually dominate the female host of the blade, Axel. If the blade sees you as its host's enemy, it will likely not hesitate to end your life."

"What happens if I fail to keep its female host alive? Will I have to fight the blade on her death?"

"I do not know what would happen in that instance. The ancient records say when a blade's host expires, it returns to Athena's original form for it. Now that so many know the archaeologist discovered something that gives its owner enormous power, hiding the blade will be next to impossible. The new host must be kept alive and trained if possible."

"You say she's still bonding with it though?"

"There are layers to the symbiosis process. She's survived the first few so far. You must take special care of her until it completes." Nyomi paced away and looked off. "If this seems too much to bother with your wolf-sitting schedule, I can have the female collected by your father. I am willing to train her myself if there's a chance to align our people with the host of the blade."

"There is no need for you to risk yourself, Mother. When have I ever refused a request from my queen?"

"Should we discuss Rian again?" Nyomi asked with a smirk.

Axel frowned and shook his head. "No, but I do have one other question. Why must we accept responsibility for the trouble this human has gotten herself into with her curiosity?"

Nyomi lifted a hand. "How can a naturally curious feline ask such a ridiculous question? That must come from your human side. This is an example of the exact selfishness I keep hoping you will one day outgrow."

"I fail to see how preferring to mind my own business is selfish. I think it's smart."

Nyomi growled in displeasure. "We could easily turn our backs and leave the blade's host to her fate, but do you want her being corrupted by those seeking to control the weapon? Do you want to fight the blade's host as an enemy one day or fight at her side as her ally? She is no doubt frightened by what has happened to her. I promise you that someone will manage to get close to her if we do not."

Axel nodded. "Again, I concede to your greater wisdom. Not being a fool, of course, I would prefer the host of the sentient blade to be an ally."

"Good. I want you to at least try to befriend the woman. Teach her to save herself if you can. That sort of benefaction is not something a human will ever forget. If we are lucky, your friendship may align her with our more noble causes in protecting this planet."

That hadn't crossed his mind, but his mother was probably right. Axel bowed his head in respect. "I will do as you ask, my queen. I will train the woman if she agrees."

"Of course, you will," Nyomi purred.

She walked back to where her son stood stoically yet mildly annoyed with her still. She lifted a hand to his handsome feline face and watched it change under her fingers to its other natural form. It was nearly a mirror image of the only human male she'd ever managed to love in all her time on Earth. His father was also the single male of any race who'd ever held her heart.

"The other children of Rodu are not like you, Axel. Your siblings were born either feline or human, but not both. Your ability to morph among the two is a great gift. I was over a thousand years old before I could shift my form. I hope one day you understand just how blessed you are to have had the ability since birth."

"If I am blessed, it is to be Queen Nyomi's beloved son. That is all I need to appreciate my happy existence."

She laughed as her hand dropped away.

"Oh, if only those words were true and not just something you incorrectly assume I want to hear. I wish you'd gotten a little more of your father's irreverence."

"Weren't you chastising me for that very thing just moments ago?"

Nyomi chuckled. "When Rodu says anything to me, at least I know his words are completely sincere. To this day, I find his directness quite refreshing. Why do you think I keep insisting he extend his human life? Your father keeps saying humans aren't meant to be so old, but it's not like I leave him old. After regenerating, he looks as young as you."

She smiled at her pleasant thoughts of Rodu as she moved away from her eldest child. "Guard the new Protector until she comes into her own, Axel. Doing so is a better use of your time than torturing that poor wolf."

Axel nodded. "Minding the wolf is merely something to keep me from being bored. I trust your judgment about the blade's host and will heed it. To the best of my ability, I will do what you have asked."

Nyomi felt her face lift in joy at his words. "Thank you, my son. May happiness find you until we see each other again."

"May happiness find you as well, Mother."

Axel lifted a hand to wave as his mother created a ball of molecular energy around herself and lifted from the ground. Only fully ascended felines possessed the gift of transporting in that manner, but such power over the elements didn't manifest until a Lyran was over three thousand years old.

As he watched her leave, it suddenly occurred to him that he actually didn't know how old his mother was. He wondered if his father knew. Come to think of it, he didn't know how old his human father was either. Their actual ages weren't something he'd ever concerned himself with knowing. His parents were, well, just his parents.

The idea of being with one person for more than a week or two alarmed him. He couldn't imagine spending several hundred years, much less a millennium, bedding only one female.

He looked down as something hit his foot. It was Max dropping the long-forgotten stick across his shoe. The wolf sat stoically at his feet with his large wolf eyes full of concern.

Axel shrugged in answer before he spoke. "Looks like I have another human pain in the ass to babysit which means you do too, Maxwell. Come on. Let's go collect her before those do-gooders at Psych Central get too involved."

—See more at donnamcdonaldauthor.com—

ROBYN'S BOOK LIST

(IN CORRECT READING ORDER)

HOT DAMNED SERIES
Fashionably Dead
Fashionably Dead Down Under
Hell on Heels
Fashionably Dead in Diapers
A Fashionably Dead Christmas
Fashionably Hotter Than Hell
Fashionably Dead and Wed
Fashionably Fanged
Fashionably Flawed
A Fashionably Dead Diary
Fashionably Forever After
Fashionably Fabulous
More coming soon…

SEA SHENANIGANS SERIES
Tallulah's Temptation
Ariel's Antics
Misty's Mayhem
Madison's Mess

SHIFT HAPPENS SERIES
Ready to Were
Some Were in Time
No Were To Run
Were Me Out
Where We Belong

MAGIC AND MAYHEM SERIES
Switching Hour
Witch Glitch
A Witch in Time
Magically Delicious
A Tale of Two Witches
Three's A Charm
Switching Witches

HANDCUFFS AND HAPPILY EVER AFTERS SERIES
How Hard Can it Be?
Size Matters
Cop a Feel

If after reading all the above you are still wanting more adventure and zany fun, read *Pirate Dave and His Randy Adventures*, the romance novel budding novelist Rena was helping wicked Evangeline write in *How Hard Can It Be?*

Warning: Pirate Dave Contains Romance Satire, Spoofing, and Pirates with Two Pork Swords.

ABOUT ROBYN PETERMAN

Robyn Peterman writes because the people inside her head won't leave her alone until she gives them life on paper.

Her addictions include laughing really hard with friends, shoes (the expensive kind), Target, Coke Zero Cherry with extra ice in a Styrofoam cup, bejeweled reading glasses, her kids, her super-hot hubby and collecting stray animals.

A former professional actress with Broadway, film and T.V. credits, she now lives in the South with her family and too many animals to count.

Writing gives her peace and makes her whole, plus having a job where you can work in your underpants works really well for her. You can leave Robyn a message via the Contact Page and she'll get back to you as soon as her bizarre life permits! She loves to hear from her fans!

Fun Ways To Connect With Robyn
www.robynpeterman.com
robyn@robynpeterman.com

Printed in Great Britain
by Amazon